The Croaker

A RINEHART SUSPENSE NOVEL

A RINEHART SUSPENSE NOVEL

John Creasey
as Gordon Ashe

The Croaker

✝ ✝
✝
✝ ✝

HOLT, RINEHART AND WINSTON
New York   Chicago   San Francisco

Preface

My first great hero, as a boy, was Bulldog Drummond, Sapper's famous character, a kind of gentleman James Bond of the twenties. My second was Edgar Wallace, with his cops and robbers fighting with nothing barred.

So it was perhaps not surprising that I wanted to write like Sapper and Wallace.

It soon became obvious that I wasn't the new Edgar Wallace, but one day in 1937—I remember it well because the previous day I'd finished a book that had taken three whole days and I really should have taken a day off—I plunged into a Bulldog Drummond type of book.

There was only one snag: my hero would *not* behave like Bulldog Drummond. In fact any likeness was no more than superficial. But what did emerge after three and a half days, however, was a book with a character named Patrick Dawlish, who rather appealed to me. Fifty-five books later, he still does.

The Croaker, called in England *The Speaker* for reasons which will become obvious to any reader, revealed qualities in Dawlish which are still evident, I hope and believe, in the latest in the series, *A Rabble of Rebels.* In whatever guise he appears, private eye, intelligence agent, or VIP policeman, he's much the same man. Matured, I hope, but the same.

The Croaker was revised a few years ago for English re-

v

print, and is not therefore presented here in its raw original version. It was first published in England under the pen name of Gordon Ashe—Ashe being the hamlet where I then lived. I made a nostalgic return about a year ago; the hamlet hasn't changed, either.

Bodenham, Wiltshire
September, 1972

The Croaker

A RINEHART SUSPENSE NOVEL

1

Visit by Night

The little man clambered through the window, hardly daring to breathe, and stretched out his right foot for the drainpipe that would take him to safety. Outside the wind was howling, although the stars were bright in their heavens and a crescent moon was shedding a silvery light which would reveal him if keepers were prowling nearby. He was thinking of the moon, the stars, and the diamonds in his coat pocket, of the police, the girl he had robbed, and the drainpipe. Most of all of the drainpipe. He kept trying to find it, but his foot would not gain purchase, and as he lowered himself farther from the sill he slipped.

He gasped, and clutched wildly with his right hand. Even when he was hanging with his two hands safely on the sill, his heart was pumping. He had forgotten everything but the drainpipe and the fact that he had just cried out aloud.

Slip Deacon started to perspire.

That slip had been nearly fatal, and he would have died as he lived—up to his nickname. Beneath him was a sixty-foot drop, for he was on the fourth floor of the Towers. The thought of the nearness of death made him hot. The cry had been suicidal.

For the first time in his life Slip Deacon was burgling a house on somebody else's behalf. He had taken orders and had done his best to obey them for a simple reason: he was afraid of the man who had given them.

Slip knew him as the Croaker.

Slip also knew that in a certain vernacular to croak meant to die or to kill. Hadn't he seen dead men who had been given orders by the Croaker and refused to carry them out? Wasn't he one of a hundred sneak-thiefs who were terrified of the Croaker? Had he not lived in fear of the Croaker for years, scared that every strange visitor to his two rooms was a messenger from the Croaker?

The call had come that morning. The orders, delivered by a strange, shadowy-looking man whose face had seemed the face of a ghoul, had been to visit Rendle Towers, near Dorking, and to force an entry to the east side middle window on the fourth floor. In the room would be a girl and some jewels, and the Croaker had asked for the jewels.

Slip had come, had found no guards nor watchmen, had discovered the room and the girl and the diamonds, and now, but for that slip, he would have been halfway out of the grounds.

He released the sill with his right hand and reached the pipe. He tested his weight on the lead and found it strong enough.

As he did so something closed round it. For the second time that night his major sensation was one of extreme cold. He stared upward, into a face that looked very pale in the moonlight, and a pair of smiling eyes.

Smiling eyes. The grip on his wrist was like steel.

Slip stayed where he was, automatically keeping his purchase on the pipe, working up for the moment when he could twist his hand away and shin down. He had felt afraid a moment before, but now that the emergency was here he was capable of facing it.

"Coming?" asked the man in the window.

Slip had had many experiences, from a winter on Dartmoor to a suite at the Melford Hotel, but never one like this. For without appearing to exert any effort the man with the smile and the deep voice hauled him up. Slip found himself held in one strong hand, rising toward the window of the room he had just left. He was dangling over that sixty-foot drop.

"Careful!—careful, mister; that's a long way down, that is!"

"Just relax," said the man in the window cheerfully. "I wouldn't like to drop you, but strange things happen to struggling men. Up she comes, here we go . . ."

Slip found himself level with the window, and still held in mid-air and at arm's length by a single arm and hand. It was true that he weighed only a hundred and twenty, but this filled him with awe of the man's strength. He forgot even the Croaker.

"Just a little bit farther," said the man at the window, "and you're all set for a comfortable night's sleep, if the local station has good beds. You don't know, I suppose?"

"Mis-*ter!*" moaned Slip, "I never did it befaw, I swear. I—— Ach!"

Just that and no more.

The man at the window felt the heavy weight of the body, the dead weight in fact, and saw the way the thief's eyes fluttered. There was something horrible in that final, almost resigned, gasp of "Ach!," as though a pain had taken the thief completely by surprise.

The man in the window supported his right hand with his left, and pulled the thief into the room. As he came, the string of diamonds dropped, and what was much more important, some drops of blood spattered the carpet.

The girl he had robbed, clad in a dressing gown now, and standing with her hand on the electric switch, stared at her diamonds and the thief. The man, no longer by the window, stood like a blond Atlas, staring at the specks of blood at the corners of the little man's mouth. Then he turned round abruptly.

"Sorry, Dee, but he's gone a long journey. Slip downstairs and call Dicker, will you? Tell him to come in first."

The girl he called Dee opened the door and stepped into the passage. The blond young man heard her footsteps, and when she started down the stairs he switched off the light and moved toward the window.

The moon was shining with the stars over a peaceful scene, and the only things that moved were the trees and the shrubs in the wind. Against the lightish green of the lawn and lightish yellow of the gravel drive he could see nothing. And then he heard a car start up. He saw it moving, long, lean, rakish-looking at the end of the drive.

"*Got* you!" snapped the blond man named Pat. He made no bones about getting through the window, and his long legs enabled him to find the drainpipe. He went down, barking his knees and his shins. His face, a peculiarly handsome one but for a broken nose, was set grimly, but his blue eyes were shining.

He reached the ground with a five-foot drop, and raced toward the rear of the house. He heard the car change gear in the distance, and knew that the only time its driver need change gear was in turning right from the road that led to the Towers into the main London-Dorking highway.

He had his keys in his hand. It could have taken him only thirty seconds to have the engine of a Jaguar ticking over, and another thirty to reach the drive.

There was only one thing in his mind—to catch the man who had killed the little thief.

Until that evening he had never knowingly seen the thief,

and never been mixed up in murder, but he had always been a man of sudden whims and abrupt decisions.

Foot right down, head well back, the wind rushing past his blond hair, and his blue eyes shining like agate, he raced onward, while the car ahead touched seventy miles an hour, and the Jaguar passed seventy-five with its needle still creeping upward.

Seventy-five—six—seven—eighty. *God!*

For another car seemed to come out of the blue, and the blond young man saw it when it was less than thirty yards away. It was stationary, almost in the middle of the road, but the gap on the left was slightly wider than that on the right.

Dawlish held his breath and swung the wheel.

The rear of the stationary car flashed past, the four front wheels were level, and the bank on the side of the road obligingly sloped a little. The Jaguar bumped, all but turned over, careered on, and left the other car behind.

The road narrowed just ahead.

Dawlish wrenched at his brakes, sending the tires screeching and the brake lining protesting. He half rose in his seat as the car jolted to a standstill, and then very gently and very gracefully he left the seat altogether and went flying over the wheel. The coolness which had often saved him from a broken collarbone on the rugby field came to his aid. He met the ground with his shoulder. A stab of pain so excruciating that he cried out seemed to wrench his arm from its socket; then the rest of his body hit the roadway and he felt a strange sensation of peace.

As he lay there dead to the world, something moved between the trees lining the road. A small man, wrapped up so that only his nose showed above his coat collar and beneath his hat brim, reached the outstretched body, glanced down into Dawlish's face, said "bloody fool," and turned away. He went

5

to the stationary small car and spent sixty seconds turning it so that he could drive along the road. One direction was impossible, because of the wrecked Jaguar, but the driver of the little car did not seem to let it worry him.

He drove past the gates of Rendle Towers five minutes later, saw lights blazing all over the building, and chuckled. It was an unpleasant chuckle, but it was nothing like a croak.

2

Inspector Trivett Complains

"I said," said Detective-Inspector Trivett of the Surrey Constabulary, "hurry. Or are you always tired?"

"Can't do the impossible," grumbled Sergeant Munk.

"Don't answer me back." Trivett, who was in evening dress, was not feeling in the best of tempers. "I'll report you for insolence, impertinence, insubordination, and incapacity if you don't move that needle past fifty."

"What'jer want—suicide?" muttered Munk.

Detective-Inspector Trivett eased his collar. There were few things he would have preferred at the moment to wringing Munk's neck, but Munk was right, for fifty on that road was faster than safety allowed, and Munk was a good, solid, dependable man.

Trivett changed the subject.

"How far to go?"

"Three mile 'n a bit."

"Who took the message at the station?"

"I did, sir."

"Who telephoned?"

Before Munk answered, the police car had rounded a sharp bend. Less than thirty yards ahead of them was a wreck, and Munk narrowly avoided adding to it. He wrenched at the brakes and brought the Morris to a standstill three feet from the blond head of a man who was lying very still.

For five seconds Munk and Detective-Inspector Trivett sat quite still. Then Munk moved.

"The last time *I* do more than fifty along here. Think he's dead?"

"I don't know." Trivett slipped from the Morris and hurried to the outstretched figure. He moved faster than Munk, for he was long and thin, whereas the sergeant was corpulent.

"He's all right," said Trivett. "I'll move him to the side of the road. You pass that bend and stop the others."

Munk stepped to the bend in the road, swinging a torch in his right hand. The second police car, with the cameramen, the fingerprint experts, and the surgeon—with luck—would be coming any moment, for when he had received an urgent phone call from Rendle Towers, with mention of murder, he had moved quickly.

Trivett lifted the blond young man to the side of the road, exerting all his strength, for the man was heavy. A quick inspection told him that the worst damage was a broken collar-bone, and there was even a chance that it was no more than a dislocation.

Trivett had a vague idea that he had seen the man before but he could not remember where. One of the young bloods of the neighborhood probably.

He reminded himself as he cut the coat away from the injured shoulder that this was to have been the night of all nights. In fact—he smiled suddenly, revealing himself to be a good-looking if somewhat saturnine man of thirty-five or thereabouts—it *had* been a night of nights for him. Grace had said "yes."

Then Munk and his message had come. Munk, for once, had been flustered. Murder had been reported at the Towers, home of Sir Jeremy Pinkerton, and the local police, with the exception of William Trivett, held the baronet in awe.

Grace had her folks to go home with. A queer life, a policeman's. For the first time in three months he had been able to go to a dance with Grace, for the first time in three years he had asked the all-important question, heard the more important answer, and then—presto!—an urgent summons to a murdered man and a mess like this in the middle of the road.

Where *had* he seen him before?

Trivett felt the collarbone and shoulder, and decided it was a dislocation that could be put right easily. Should he do it himself, or wait for Mendor, the surgeon? Probably Mendor would have something sarcastic to say if he tried his hand.

Trivett made the young man as comfortable as he could, saw that there was a speck of blood on his boiled-shirt front, scowled, and straightened up. As he did so he heard the sound of an approaching car engine, and by the time he had reached the bend in the road the second police car had drawn up.

Trivett took control immediately.

"Four of you, with Munk, shift the car in front. Doctor, there's a chap here wants attention. Would you mind?"

"For you, yes," said Doctor Horace Mendor. "Which reminds me that I have to congratulate you. I have always admired Grace—from a distance, of course, from a respectable distance!"

"I hope so," said Trivett, less heartily than he intended.

He had never liked Mendor. His dislike had started when he had first learned that the police surgeon's name was Horace. Mendor looked like a Giuseppe or at least a Juan—a rather tall, thin, dark-haired man, sallow of skin and with the shining eyes of the South. There was Mendor's suave way of talking, too. And how *had* he learned about Grace and him?

Yet Trivett was forced to admire the way in which he pushed the arm back after pronouncing a dislocation and slight concussion. In five minutes the blond man was bandaged and comfortable, and the doctor straightened up.

"We will take him home."

"Home. Where?"

"Why, the Towers, of course. Don't tell me you haven't recognized him. The hair and the mouth and chin, you see— Pinkerton to the life!"

Trivett was seeing that now.

Sir Jeremy Pinkerton, of Rendle Towers, possessed a lot of things, including relatives. Trivett remembered hearing that a nephew had recently put in an appearance at the Towers, a young man with a reputation at sport and big game. Patrick, that was the name, although there was a surname about somewhere. He was not a Pinkerton, but he was said to be the old man's only male relative.

The Jaguar was not such a wreck as it might have been, although it would need a towtruck to get it off the side of the road. Two of the policemen came up at Trivett's command and lifted Dawlish gently into the larger car. Trivett took the wheel of the Morris, Mendor sat beside him, and Munk was in the rear with a mass of cameras and other impedimenta.

It would be only a matter of minutes before they reached the Towers. Trivett forced his engagement to the back of his mind, and even forgot his annoyance with Mendor.

There had been a car chase, or so Trivett reasoned, and the blond man had been in it. Which was good for him, but it suggested that there had been an outsider in the affair of the Towers, which was bad for Trivett.

He was frowning when the cars pulled up outside the majestic main doors of the towers. Practically every window in the big building was ablaze with light, and against some of the drawn blinds he could see the silhouettes of men and women. Mostly, Trivett soon saw, in their dressing gowns.

Supposing he worked out the times before he asked questions.

Munk had telephoned him at twelve-thirty. Say half an hour

had passed from the time the call had first been put through to the police station to the time he had left the Castle Ballroom. That meant that the latest hour for the crime to have been committed was midnight.

Trivett entered the large hall of the Towers. He recognized the two footmen who opened the door, and ignored them. That was as well, for the man who was advancing toward him would have engaged his whole attention in any case.

Sir Jeremy Pinkerton had been an eight-bottle man in his youth. He looked it. In Trivett's opinion he also looked a complete wreck. His face was swollen, his nose bulbous and blue-veined, his eyes rheumy. He suffered severely from gout, although this was one of his good periods, for he was walking with the aid of a stick, and wearing no bandages.

Trivett was forced to admire the man. He had a way with him, and Trivett unconsciously stiffened his back. Sir Jeremy might be the richest landowner about here, but the police had no undue respect for riches.

Sir Jeremy spoke in a rich, mellow voice that occasionally broke into a harsh croak or a high-pitched quaver, a thing that had always tickled Trivett until then.

"Ha. Police, eh? At last. Who's in charge?"

"Detective-Inspector Trivett," said Trivett.

"The poor devil in there needs you." Sir Jeremy waved his hand, and the "in there" might have included the heavens. But in his rheumy eyes there was a twinkle that most people except Trivett appreciated.

"And where, exactly, is 'there,'—Sir Jeremy?"

"In the small library. Welsh, show the gentleman."

No one could have slurred that "gentleman" as well as Sir Jeremy, whose foot was giving him hell and who was more than annoyed to be disturbed to learn, among other things, that a dead man was on his hands and his nephew missing.

11

Also he had discovered that his nephew had been in his prettiest niece's room at midnight.

Sir Jeremy, seventy-one and no fool, was worried, although he would never have allowed the fact to be known. He had kept one secret fairly well already—the fact that on the previous day he had received a communication from a gentleman who called himself the Croaker.

Now he was asking himself what would happen if that leaked out? He had a conscience, and it was disquieting to think that if he had told the police instead of throwing the note away, a man now dead might have been alive. On the other hand, he was a ferrety-faced little man, and probably a lot better dead.

They would see, thought Sir Jeremy, and he followed Trivett into the small library and the body of Slip Deacon.

3

Odds and Ends

"I want to remind you, Inspector, that this is a matter that must be kept strictly confidential," Pinkerton said. "Understand?"

It was almost possible to see the hairs rising at the back of Trivett's neck, and he kept his temper only with an effort. His dislike of the aristocracy as represented by Sir Jeremy Pinkerton had almost turned him Communist in the past half-hour, and several times he had only saved himself from downright rudeness by thinking of Grace, and the fact that he could keep her in greater luxury on a chief-inspector's salary.

"*Everything* handled by the police is confidential, Sir Jeremy. My report will go through the usual channels."

"Harrmph!" Sir Jeremy's voice went screeching upward. "Newspapers, eh, newspapers? Let a word of this get to the newspapers and I'll have your uniform off your back." Sir Jeremy avoided Trivett's eyes and his own gleamed. "Now, Delia, let's have the truth. Whole truth, understand?"

Miss Delia Granley smiled at Trivett and reminded him of Grace.

"Of course, Uncle. But——"

She glanced toward the door of Sir Jeremy's study, where they were sitting. At the door were two plainclothes men, and by a small table was a man in uniform with a notebook and a pencil.

She was wondering whether they need be here, Trivett told himself, and he relented a little. One thing was nearly certain; the dead man had been killed from outside, and no one inside the house knew anything about it. Delia Granley had told her story well. How she had awakened to see the man in the window, how she had hurried to the door, opened it, and found Pat standing there—or walking past—how she had whispered what had happened, and how he had handled the intruder. But when and how the man had died she could not say, only that he had appeared to go limp while Pat had been hauling him through the window.

Trivett sent the two plainclothes men out, and Delia repeated her story, which was taken down in shorthand. Sir Jeremy seemed almost disappointed about the meeting with Pat outside the room; or incredulous, Trivett wasn't sure which.

Trivett read through the statement, and Delia agreed that it was correct. Sir Jeremy scowled.

"And now what?"

"I'd like to telephone headquarters, sir, and then talk to your nephew as soon as he recovers consciousness. There's a chance that he will be able to give us some information."

"There's more than a chance that he won't," snapped Sir Jeremy, and for the first time Trivett realized that the baronet's acerbity was not reserved for policemen or men in uniform. "Why the devil did he have to go throwing himself out of the window after the men outside? Police job to catch murderers, isn't it?"

"If I may say so," said Trivett, who was stiff and formal and a changed man when he was talking with Pinkerton, "I think it was a praiseworthy effort. Mr.—er—Patrick narrowly escaped with his life, and——"

"Why don't you call him Dawlish?—that's his name," growled Sir Jeremy, and Delia knew that the old man was

14

proud of his nephew. "Well, get your telephoning done, and then come up to his room. Who's that doctor? Don't like the look of him."

"He's the police surgeon," said Trivett, hardly knowing whether to be annoyed at the implied criticism of the police or gratified that Sir Jeremy did not take to Mendor.

"Is he? A recommendation, you think?"

Trivett, preceded by a solemn-faced footman, left the small library. At the same time Pinkerton and his niece went upstairs, toward the room where Pat Dawlish had been taken.

Trivett was thoughtful about many things, and his annoyance at Pinkerton's manner was soon forgotten. He had been busy in the short time he had been at the Towers, but was convinced that this work had been purely routine, that the murderer had never set foot on the grounds. Trivett, in fact, could almost reconstruct the crime.

The burglary had been committed successfully, but Dawlish had stopped the thief's getaway. An accomplice in the grounds had preferred to see the man dead rather than caught by the police, which suggested a ruthlessness that made the detective-inspector feel uneasy.

He did not complain that the body had been moved from the room, for it was obvious it could have made no difference. The photographs of the murdered man could tell Trivett nothing more than his eyes had already done, while the fingerprints had revealed the presence of four people in the room in the past few hours. A maid, thought Trivett, the thief, Dawlish, and Miss Granley.

Had Dawlish just happened to be passing the door?

Trivett's lips twitched as he telephoned Guildford headquarters. He learned, not without surprise, that Superintendent Donovan of the Surrey C.I.D. was already on his way—men like Sir Jeremy Pinkerton could only be handled by the VIP's of the profession—and that there was talk of getting someone from the Yard.

Trivett, speaking to a chief-inspector, sounded noncommittal.

"I think that's an idea, Parsons. This isn't a local man and it's not a local job. Have you any ideas about it?"

"What kind?" asked Inspector Parsons, who was a suspicious man by nature.

"Well," said Trivett slowly, "how many thieves work in pairs with one of them prepared to shoot the moment trouble comes?"

"Not many," admitted the man at the other end of the wire. "What are you driving at?"

"Just thinking," said Trivett, "wondering whether this has anything to do with the Croaker."

There was a moment's silence at the other end, and Trivett knew that his words had taken effect. He had, in fact, been playing with the possibility that the Croaker was in this affair for some time, although he had hardly dared use the name even to himself. But the cold-bloodedness with which everything had been done—and obviously planned beforehand—brought that name vividly in front of his mind.

There was not a C.I.D. man in England who had not heard of the Croaker. Mostly in rumors, although occasionally there had been one of those round-robin letters from the Yard, in which the sobriquet had been mentioned. Trivett recalled some of them while he waited for Parsons' reaction.

Men who had been brought in after a burglary had talked, and mentioned the Croaker. Men who had been dying when the police had found them had gasped: "The Croaker." Fences who had been taken with the goods on them had muttered about the Croaker, and refused to mention the source of their ill-gotten gains.

The Croaker. . . .

His reputation was almost fantastic. Once Trivett had been inclined to scoff at the name, just as half the people in England had. But it had grown very insistent in recent weeks. Moreover, the first mention of the Croaker had been heard a year before, and a year was a long life for a rumor.

Trivett began to feel the pricking of excitement.

Supposing this was the Croaker's work—supposing he, William James Trivett, succeeded in laying the Croaker by the heels?

"I say," said Parsons, who was a mild-mannered man, "do you seriously think so?"

"I seriously think it's possible," said Trivett, jerked out of his dreams. "All right, I'll wait for Donovan. You don't know whether they have sent to the Yard, do you?"

"No. Quench is here, and I heard him muttering."

"Thanks," said Trivett, and hung up thoughtfully.

Sir Quentin Lawson was the Surrey chief constable, and Trivett needed no telling that only the magic name of Sir Jeremy Pinkerton could have brought the Chief to Guildford at that unholy hour. Things were going to move fast, and if he overlooked anything he would be in trouble.

He was in an uneasy frame of mind when he followed the footman, whose name he never learned, and whom he saw only as a long streak in knickerbockers and purple stockings, for they lived in style at the Towers. Two of his own men were with him, and he supposed Mendor was with the man Dawlish.

How was the blond young man?

Dawlish was sitting up, he saw a moment later, and taking nourishment. Now that his eyes were open, very blue and clear and filled with a merriment which seemed absurd after the crack over the head and the jolt to his shoulder, Trivett could see why Patrick Dawlish had earned fame at big-game hunting and on the sporting fields. He was clad in pink pajamas and was sitting up in bed, with several pillows stuffed behind him. Sitting on one side was Sir Jeremy, silent for once, and on the other the attractive Delia Granley.

Mendor was standing with his lean hands clasped near his gold watch chain, and smiling down at the invalid, with Sergeant Munk beside him.

Sir Jeremy jerked round.

"Ah! The man who picked you up, Patrick, Inspector Trivett."

"Munk really saved you," said Trivett, nodding toward Dawlish and pointing at the sergeant. "What can you tell us, Mr. Dawlish?"

Dawlish's only additional information was that the man had been shot while he, Dawlish, had been holding him, and that the car in which the murderers had made off had been long, lean, and rakish. As the word "rakish" came out, Trivett's head jerked up. He remembered one of the more recent letters from the Yard:

. . . the car, described as low-bodied and rakish, is believed to be a Lancia. The name of the Croaker . . .

"What's the matter?" asked Sir Jeremy.

"Just an idea," said the policeman slowly. "Well, Doctor, is there much to worry about?"

"Nothing, nothing at all," Mendor assured him. "Anything else you want me for, Inspector?"

"Nothing, thanks." Trivett nodded and the doctor made his exit, bowing and smiling, with those dark eyes of his gleaming as though at some secret joke. Trivett felt better when the door had closed, and Sir Jeremy said something that the policeman thought it wiser not to hear. He reported the impending arrival of Superintendent Donovan from Guildford, and the possibility of a Yard man putting in an appearance before long.

"Why all the fuss?" asked Pinkerton.

"It's murder," said Trivett, immediately annoyed again. "And it's obviously not a local killer, Sir Jeremy. Mr. Dawlish confirms that with the talk about the car."

"Nothing else?"

Trivett's hazel eyes were suddenly turned toward the baronet. Delia Granley told herself the policeman was unusually good-looking, and she rather liked him. He was too self-conscious, of course, but Sir Jeremy often made people feel like that.

"Why should there be, sir?"

"Come downstairs," said Pinkerton abruptly. "That is if you can spare a minute."

The door closed behind the baronet, Munk, and Trivett, and left Delia alone with Patrick Dawlish, whose smile was wearing a little thin, for his arm was painful. But Dawlish chuckled as the door snapped to.

"Jeremy's getting under that detective's skin, darling. Well, what do you think of it?"

"Oughtn't I to think it's horrible?"

"I expect you did at first, but that little man wasn't anyone to grieve about. On the other hand, it looks what the prophets would call a big job. Or doesn't it?"

"I think it does," admitted Delia. She sat on the end of Pat's bed, medium-tall, dark-haired, and with a profile that would have made Dawlish lose his heart five years ago, although now from the wisdom of his thirty years he knew better than to judge on beauty alone. "It's a pity that it happened to you, Pat. You might have pushed your name in the papers again."

"It will get there," said Dawlish sadly. "The hounds of the

press won't leave me alone, darling, and my life for the last five years will be rehashed. But listen. There was the rakish car——"

"I don't like that word."

"I don't care," beamed Dawlish. "And the smaller car that had been planted in my way. Two cars, in fact, which means there were at least two men besides our corpse on the grounds tonight. And *all* for your necklace."

He glanced at her white throat, but the necklace wasn't there. It was in the safe, where, as Sir Jeremy had said with emphasis, it should have been all the time.

Delia frowned.

"Yet it wasn't a particularly valuable one."

"How much?"

"I don't know—it was a present."

"Don't tell me you didn't have it valued," said Dawlish unkindly. "Say ten thousand?"

"Nothing like that."

"H'mm. Three men, two cars at a house with twenty servants and a dozen residents, for a necklace. Dee, my sweet, I've a hankering to be a detective, but I'm too tired at the moment. Tuck me up, will you?"

Delia Granley obliged, and slipped out of the room three minutes later. Patrick Dawlish looked to be asleep, and after his experience he needed the rest.

Meanwhile, Detective-Inspector Trivett had listened to the story of the letter from the Croaker, and could hardly conceal his satisfaction. He was prepared to forgive Sir Jeremy his unpleasant manners, for this confirmed his theory, and the theory had been passed over to Parsons at Guildford: in short, it had collaboration, and he had proved his perspicacity. He was anxious, too, to have the whole story pat before Donovan arrived.

"You've had nothing of this nature before, sir?"

"I haven't," said Pinkerton, seriously. "Sorry I didn't keep the letter, Trivett. Thought it a damfool joke. Postmark London W.11."

"The odd thing," said Trivett, scratching his cheek, "is that it was all for a single diamond necklace. It just doesn't seem important enough, Sir Jeremy. You've put the necklace away?"

"Yes, in the strong-room. Like to see it again?"

"I would," said Trivett.

They collected Sergeant Munk and a plainclothes man, by name Sanders, from outside the room where they had been talking, and went downstairs to the strong-room. Sir Jeremy's strong-room was in the cellars, and Trivett—who had seen the place once before—was impressed by the baronet's precautions. The Pinkerton family jewels were always kept in the vault, and only a madman would have taken risks to get anything from there.

To reach the strong-room they went by stairs that were wide at the top but gradually narrowing. There was only a dim glow of light from below, and Sir Jeremy growled:

"All the lights ought to be on; I'll talk to Graham about this. Mind that step. I——"

And then Sir Jeremy felt the detective-inspector grab his wrist and hurl him downward, sensed Trivett had dropped to his knees, heard the grunt from Sergeant Munk, and out of the corner of his eyes saw the flashes of flame coming from somewhere ahead of him.

Someone was in the strong-room—and the someone was shooting!

4

Mr. Dawlish Convalesces

Trivett had not dreamed of the possibility of this happening, but he was automatically on the alert, and his eyes were used to semidarkness. He had seen the shroudy figure of the man ten yards ahead of him and had recognized the gun in his hand. He had moved so quickly that Pinkerton was still breathless. Now, with Munk, he saw the flashes of flame and heard the bullets plopping.

The truth seared through Trivett.

The burglary and the diamond necklace had been a blind. Somehow someone had forced an entry to the house and was working at the strong-room now, someone who cared nothing for the power of the police, and who was prepared to take tremendous risks. He had no time for thinking more than that; he had no time even for fear. He did have time to wish that he had a gun; then, gathering every ounce of strength, he hurled himself forward.

He saw two stabs of flame and felt something tear through his shoulder, but before he realized the extent of the pain, he had crashed on his man. He heard a gasp, and struck out with his uninjured right arm, catching the man beneath the chin.

Bedlam was reigning in the cellars now.

Trivett could see nothing, but he heard men's voices and the occasional *hiss* as a bullet spat out from a silenced automatic. He heard Munk's voice, raised to its highest pitch, others that seemed to come from a long way off, and then, as he straightened out with the unconscious figure of the man beside him, he saw the gun that was still clutched in the man's right hand.

Trivett reached out, and as his fingers closed about the steel he saw two vague, shadowy figures rushing toward the stairs, and he touched the trigger of the gun. Once—twice! A high-pitched scream seemed to rend the very air, and Trivett saw one of the marauders pitch forward on his face. But the other was still moving.

Trivett fired again, but there was a harmless click. He hauled himself up, and as he did so the main lights in the strong-room vault were switched on.

The sight that met his eyes seemed a fantasy.

His own victim was stretched out, with his face very pale and an ugly bruise on his chin. The man he had shot was lying close to Sir Jeremy, whose left cheek was bleeding freely, and who looked exhausted. Halfway up the stairs was Munk, grappling with the third marauder. Munk was fighting fiercely, but he looked as if he would have to give way any minute.

Trivett gritted his teeth and went forward. As he reached the foot of the stairs he saw the three men who were standing on top—servants, and a policeman from Dorking. They were scared or hypnotized, but Trivett used his gun as a club and crashed it down on Munk's opponent's head. A single gasp, and the man slid from Munk's grasp. The only sound on the stairs was the heavy breathing of Munk and himself as they stood staring like statues at the chaos below.

Trivett's head was whirling, his shoulder was a splitting devil, but all the time there was a tremendous elation in his mind. He'd made it, he'd saved the strong-room. He . . .

He fainted, suddenly and completely, and it was twenty minutes before he came round.

"And the unofficial postmortem," said Mr. Patrick Dawlish cheerfully, "is about to commence. How's the shoulder, Trivett?"

"Fair," said Detective-Inspector Trivett with a grunt. "How's yours?"

"Bloody," said Mr. Dawlish just as cheerfully. He gazed around the room—the large library at the Towers, on the ground floor—and regarded the assembled company. Delia Granley, because of her diamond necklace, was the only woman present. She was sitting in an easy chair and showing rather a lot of knee. Sir Jeremy Pinkerton, with his bandages hiding his veins and most of his rheumy eyes, was propped up on a settee. Trivett was sitting stiffly opposite Dawlish, and both had a left arm in a sling. Sergeant Munk, that rotund, gloomy-looking, and beefy-faced man, was staring blankly ahead of him, and a large, immaculate, florid-faced detective named Donovan was standing by the window.

Superintendent Donovan felt reasonably satisfied at the way events had turned out, and so did the lean man sitting nearest the door. He was not unlike Trivett to look at, a man of perhaps forty-five, with light gray eyes set in a dark, almost saturnine face. He had the most pleasant voice Delia had ever heard, and a thin black line of moustache that made him altogether a storybook hero.

Thus Superintendent Charleton of Scotland Yard.

It was nearly three o'clock on the afternoon following the astonishing affair at the Towers, and this, as Patrick Dawlish said cheerfully, was the postmortem. Theories, facts, and possibilities had been discussed, and at this conference they would be marshaled into some order.

"It would seem," said Charleton in that very deep voice,

"that the Croaker planned the job very carefully, Sir Jeremy. He warned you, and he made the attempt on the necklace, and quite obviously the necklace was a blind."

But for the bandages, Sir Jeremy would have made a biting comment, for Charleton was not being original.

"Whether the man Deacon had been murdered or not, the theft of the necklace would have been discovered and the police brought here. While the police were busy upstairs the Croaker's men would come in, for they could—and they did —come in the guise of policemen or detectives. On each of the three men was an identity card showing him to be a member of the Surrey Force, which proves that the Croaker was very careful indeed. But for Trivett's idea of going to see the strong-room, most of your jewels would be in other hands by now."

"Ha!" growled Sir Jeremy.

Superintendent Charleton smiled at Delia.

"As it is, nothing at all is missing. Only Deacon suffered for his pains—and, of course, the three men who were captured. For the first time," added the Superintendent, fingering his thin line of moustache and smiling, "the Croaker has suffered a severe setback."

"Shouldn't try to rob me," growled Sir Jeremy, who wished the man from Scotland Yard would be less pedantic.

"Any luck with the three prisoners?" asked Dawlish, who had been quiet for a long time—for him. He looked absurdly handsome, despite his broken nose, and the September sun shining through the window caught his blond hair.

"Not yet," said Charleton. "Only one of them is fully conscious—Trivett shoots straight." Charleton smiled at the detective-inspector, who felt that promotion was a certainty now. He had saved something like a hundred thousand pounds' worth of jewelry, probably one or two lives, and he had persuaded three of the Croaker's men to interview a police-station cell. They would doubtless go one further and visit Dartmoor before the year was out, and it was safe to say that, for the first time since the rumors of his activities had first reached the ears of the police, the Croaker had had his knuckles rapped. It was a very satisfactory situation indeed.

Dawlish, on a stiff-backed chair because of his shoulder, crossed his legs.

"Light me a cigarette, Dee darling. Charleton—there's been a lot of talk about the Croaker. Who is he?"

"I'd give a fortune to know his name or get his photograph," said Charleton soberly. "All I can tell you, Mr. Dawlish, is that he can be considered the most dangerous operating criminal in England today. Dangerous because of his ruthlessness, and I assure you I am not exaggerating."

"I can guess that," admitted Dawlish. "Nothing at all known about him?"

"Nothing at all. And I'm afraid that the three men caught here last night won't talk."

"Why not?"

"They'll be scared of the Croaker."

"And so is the Yard?"

"Worried more than scared, Mr. Dawlish." Charleton stood up and bowed to Pinkerton. "I don't think you need worry about any further trouble, Sir Jeremy, but I'll ask Mr. Donovan to leave men here in case of accidents. Is there anything else you'd like?"

"I'd like some peace," growled Sir Jeremy, squinting from beneath his bandages. "Where's Trivett? Ah! Getting married soon, I'm told."

Trivett went red under the ears.

"I hope so, Sir Jeremy."

"Good. I'd like to see the gel. Make sure she's worth it. Damned plucky piece of work last night, Trivett. Good-bye, and drop in some time."

Detective-Inspector Trivett took the baronet's hand with something like stupefaction, shook it, and found himself leaving the room with the other policemen. He was revising his opinion of the aristocracy, and Sir Jeremy Pinkerton in particular.

Several things of varying importance happened in the next three months.

The Croaker, after his setback, was quieter than usual, and certain people in the East End of London breathed more easily. Slip Deacon was buried without pomp. Three men were sent to Dartmoor from the Surrey Assizes for sentences totaling thirty-one years, for all of them had been armed, ensuring severe sentences. Detective-Inspector William Trivett became a chief-inspector, and, exactly three months from the day when he had taken a chance and hurled himself at a gunman, was appointed to Scotland Yard, taking Sergeant Munk with him. A young man named Grayson proposed successfully to Delia, Sir Jeremy's prettiest niece, and married her almost too quickly for decency. And—last but a long way from least important—Patrick Dawlish convalesced from his hurts and —as he told Dee plaintively—from his broken heart.

But while he lingered in the valley of depression he thought a great deal, and the more he thought, the more often a name ran through his mind. The name of the Croaker. He was intrigued by the Croaker, and he wanted to interview the gentleman. More, he would give a great deal to see the Croaker where the police wanted him—dead or behind bars.

It had been his firm opinion that there had been grounds for a murder charge against the three men found at the Towers, but the police were convinced to the contrary, and had preferred to make sure of long terms of imprisonment to a possible "not guilty" on a murder charge. That opinion made him

27

wonder whether the police were really ruthless enough in their dealings with the Croaker.

The Croaker, he told himself, could fight regulations and a court of law because he knew what to expect from them. Was it just possible that unorthodox methods would be more effective?

Dawlish thought they would. After the marriage of Delia Granley there was nothing to keep him at the Towers, and he took a flat in London and proposed, in the opinion of Sir Jeremy Pinkerton, to throw his money away.

"But you've got plenty," Dawlish assured his relative. "Or am I to be cut off?"

"You young devil, you know you won't! Why go to London? I'm lonely down here. Getting old too."

"You don't want my company," said Patrick Dawlish gently. "You just want to make sure that I'm behaving. Pinky, listen. That's if you can keep a secret?"

"Damn and blast you!" roared Sir Jeremy, ending absurdly on a quaver. "What's the matter? Still thinking of the Croaker, after three months?"

Mr. Dawlish chuckled and patted his uncle's head.

"You're no fool," he admitted. "Yes, I'm still thinking of the Croaker. In fact, I'm going after the Croaker."

"Damned young idiot!" growled Sir Jeremy, and then he quavered again, quite by accident. "All the luck in the world, my boy. Don't spare expense. I'd like to do something."

"You keep out of this," said Mr. Dawlish. "It's a job for the young 'uns. Sorry I can't keep it all in the family, but I'll keep you posted on developments."

"When are you starting?"

"Tomorrow," said Mr. Dawlish, pressing his uncle's shoulder. "There'll be four of us, all men sound in wind and limb, and smart—nearly as smart as me. By the way, don't you know the Home Secretary?"

"You know I do," growled Sir Jeremy. "Why?"

"Use your influence for a reprieve, won't you?" asked Mr. Patrick Dawlish. "Because I'm going to carry a gun for a little while to come, in the hope of croaking the Croaker."

5

And Goes to a Party

Chief-Inspector Trivett, now of Scotland Yard, shared a room with Sergeant Munk. Not because he was any better than the other chief-inspectors, four of whom shared an office, but because the room was next to Superintendent Charleton's, and all three were working against the Croaker.

If the Croaker had been singing on a lower key he had been singing effectively enough.

He had a small personal gang and used a hundred or a thousand outsiders for his purposes. As with Slip Deacon. The Croaker singled out a crook to do a job for him and relied on the man's fear to persuade him to accomplish the job well. He used a man just once and no more. In that way he was able to be sure that no one but his own select circle of friends knew much about him, or the operations of his organization. In that way also he made sure that no one could give to the police any worthwhile information.

Trivett had discussed this matter with Charleton one morning ten days after his transfer from Dorking, and afterward he was sitting in his office and making unpleasant remarks about Munk's middle. It was a middle in a thousand and had already been the subject of ribaldry at the Yard. Munk bore it all with resignation, for he was secretly proud to be at Westminster.

"Think we'll ever get him?" he asked glumly. Munk was always glum, and his brick-red face suited the mood.

"One day, certain," said Trivett, who looked younger and more carefree; that morning he had received a letter from Grace. "The sooner the better, because—— Damn the thing!"

He lifted the receiver off the telephone, frowned, smiled and chuckled. Then:

"Yes, come along by all means. You're alone?"

"If you mean I haven't brought Pinky, I'm alone," said Patrick Dawlish at the other end of the wire. "Do I come straight up?"

"You'll have to sign a form," said Trivett. "I'll send Munk down to meet you at the door. How long will you be?"

"Give me fifteen minutes."

Trivett explained in two-syllable words to Munk that Patrick Dawlish would like to renew their acquaintance, and sent Munk to meet him. Certainly Dawlish looked blonder and more absurdly handsome than ever, and his silver-grays—despite a chill December—seemed to brighten the office. He dropped his hat and stick on the desk and his gloves in his lap, and offered cigarettes.

"You haven't changed, Trivett, but the Sergeant's getting fatter. How's things?"

"Fine," said Trivett. "What's brought you here?"

"Mutual love and respect," said Mr. Dawlish.

"Don't fool," said Trivett. "Has anything happened to worry you?"

Dawlish stopped smiling and frowned.

"Well, no; I've an urge."

"What kind?"

Dawlish scratched his chin, and then drew a deep breath.

"It's like this, Inspector. The Croaker has been on my mind and I can't get him off. I've been trying to get a line on the gentleman, but I haven't succeeded. I thought perhaps you——"

"You haven't learned anything?" asked Trivett quickly.

31

"Only that the purlieus down East are scared of the Croaker," said Dawlish. "I've visited a hundred and thirty-two pubs in the past ten days, and whenever I mentioned that name everyone curled up. Fact. But perhaps you'd heard about that?"

"More than once," admitted Trivett. "And you seriously want to try your hand?"

"Seriously is only half the word."

"H'mm. Unofficially?"

"Strictly."

"H'm-h'mm," said William Trivett, and he glanced at Munk. Munk was nodding, and it didn't mean he was sleepy. There was a sudden, hardly explicable, tension in that small office, and Pat Dawlish knew he had struck a good day. Trivett went on: "Well, I can't promise you anything. But among other things we've learned in the past few days that there's a gaming salon being run in Clarge Street——"

"By a man named Greet. Don't I know it!"

Trivett leaned forward, his hazel eyes gleaming.

"You're a member?"

"Unofficially, I'm a member," Dawlish admitted.

"You know Greet?"

"I've met him."

"Do you know the syndicate that's running the show?"

"I don't," admitted Dawlish. He wriggled his vast shoulders as if to show how sorry he was.

"That doesn't matter much," said Inspector Trivett. "We can get men inside that place without much trouble, but they're always spotted. We could close the place up, but——"

Dawlish shifted his position.

"You think the Croaker's involved?"

"We've heard rumors, " admitted Trivett, "and we want to go carefully. Will you go there tonight and see what you can find?"

"I will," said Patrick Dawlish. "I'll take a party in case of accidents. But what's this syndicate you mention?"

Trivett, who had already reached his decision, took a sheet of plain paper from a pad and scribbled five names and addresses on it. He did not speak, but passed the names over the table. Dawlish read them, his eyes widening. Slowly:

"And *these* fellows are backing the club?"

"It's a purely private affair, run for their pleasure," said Trivett. "But two M.P.'s, a peer, and two millionaires make a fairly imposing show. I'd like to know more about their activities at the Greet Club, Dawlish, and if you can give me information I'll be grateful."

Patrick Dawlish stood up to his full six feet three.

"It's as good as done," he said, "and I'll be seeing you. But you won't have any of your men there tonight?"

"No, you'll be alone as far as I'm concerned."

"Fine," said Mr. Dawlish, and he collected his hat, stick, and gloves and left the Yard.

Exactly forty minutes later Dawlish was sitting in the lounge of the Cranton Club waving to a waiter. The Cranton Club, at that time of the day, was chock full, and most of its occupants were middle-aged to old. The vast Dawlish in his silvery gray suit struck a false note, but as the waiter approached it was obvious that he was getting near a distinguished client.

"Good morning, Mr. Dawlish. Beer?"

"As always, " said Dawlish. "And, Sam, I'm expecting some friends. Messrs. Cutter, Rawling, and Beresford."

"Mr. Beresford, sir, is over there talking to his father; Mr. Cutter said he'd be coming back; and Mr. Rawling hasn't been in this morning, sir."

"Tell 'em I'm here," said Dawlish, who looked as though he had hardly heard what Sam had told him.

But Sam heard, for within five minutes two beers preceded

two gentlemen and reached Dawlish's table. They greeted him solemnly and said, "Here's how!" before sitting down. Mr. Beresford—Edward, and sometimes known as Ted—was nearly as large as Dawlish, with a peculiarly bulldoggish face. Mr. Cutter, who had returned as Sam had left Dawlish's table, was a small man by comparison, and generally thought a bit of a clown, perhaps because of his buttonhole, for he was a specialist in buttonholes, and it was said that he knew more about leading ladies than any other man in London.

Mr. Beresford was dressed in navy blue and Cutter in dark gray. To complete the funereal note, Mr. Anthony Rawling appeared in full mourning equipment as the others settled down. The Christian name of Mr. Cutter was Wishart, but no one had ever been known to use it. Folks called him Cutts.

Sam, watching from afar off, brought Rawling's beer, and Dawlish leaned forward. He was smiling, but it was an odd fact that he looked serious.

"Friends," he said, "news. We've a date tonight at Greet's in Clarge Street. We're to take special notice of Greet and these five johnnies."

He put the list that he had obtained from Trivett on the table, and the others ran down it quickly. They were as surprised as Dawlish had been.

The names read:

> *Sir Hugo Pelisse, Bart.*
> *Mr. Ronald Renway, M.P.*
> *Mr. Arthur Golding, M.P.*
> *Sir Charles Faversham.*
> *Mr. Horatio Fayre.*

Beresford, cocking his massive head on one side, looked skeptical.

"I don't think there's a thing to it, do you?"

"False alarm," growled Mr. Cutter, whose voice was a perpetual dirge.

"Where'd it come from?" asked Tony Rawling, and Dawlish patted his back, while Sam brought the replenishments.

"It came from the Yard, and this quintet runs the Greet Club. Why and how the Croaker is suspected to be connected I don't know and I don't care, but we're going to a party. And listen, Ted . . ."

"H'mm?"

"We're going on business. It's a mixed club and there will probably be faces worth looking at, but keep sober."

"All because," said Beresford bitterly, "I once helped a girl who was tight into a taxi." He grinned, and his homely face looked oddly attractive. "All right, Pat. But—are you seriously expecting anything to happen?"

"No, I'm just hoping."

It was a sheer coincidence that Sir Hugo Pelisse, the first on the list, should choose that moment to enter the Cranton Club, for the first time in three months. Pelisse was a tall, soldierly looking man with a ferocious expression and a drum major's bark. He was not popular. He walked sharply through the lounge and reached the door leading to the dining room—it was nearly one o'clock—and then he stopped.

He stopped so suddenly that a dozen people looking at him wondered what had happened. And then Pat Dawlish let out a roar that reached the street outside and raced toward the baron, while Sir Hugo Pelisse toppled forward, slowly and gently, to the floor.

6

Business

Silence settled on the Cranton Club and no one moved. Even Beresford, Cutter, and Rawling stayed where they were, as though afraid of what might happen next. All of them were thinking the same thing—that indirectly the Croaker had been connected with Sir Hugo Pelisse, and now Pelisse was lying in a queer, outstretched position on the floor, with Dawlish feeling for his heart.

It was hardly necessary.

There was blood on Dawlish's hand when he took it away, and there was an audible gasp through the room. Then a dozen men moved forward at once, and someone called: "Police!" Feurier, the club's manager, appeared as if from nowhere.

"Mr. Dawlish, he——"

"Shot while we were watching," said Dawlish. Few people there recognized his voice, for was harsher than it had ever been in his life before. "Have the doors closed, as soon as I've gone. Tony, keep the crowd back. Ted, telephone the Yard and ask for Trivett."

"But you——" Monsieur Feurier started.

"I'm going out on business," said Dawlish. "Cutts, come with me. Find a doctor if there isn't one here, Feurier, but it'll do no good. Nor will the closed doors, unless you hurry."

The tension that had settled over the Cranton Club grew worse as Dawlish strode toward the door; Cutter, small and comparatively insignificant, went with him. Dawlish seemed to be looking ahead, but his eyes were alert, and as he reached the door he muttered:

"Faversham's here, and so is Renway, both on the list. A gathering of the clans, I wonder?"

"What's your move now?"

"I don't know, but Pelisse never travels without his car. We'll find where he's been this morning."

A porter hesitated as the two men reached the door. But before he could suggest that they should stay inside, Dawlish was on the porch. Dawlish had a habit of moving when he seemed to be standing still.

"Keep the doors closed and make sure no one comes out," he said. "Cutts, there's the car. Do you know Pelisse well?"

"Fairly."

"Is that his regular chauffeur?"

"One of them."

Dawlish reached the gray Rolls standing in the courtyard of the Cranton, and nodded to the chauffeur, a man who looked too small to handle a big car. "Sir Hugo's man?"

"Yessir."

"I'm afraid you've a shock coming. There's been an accident inside, and——"

The chauffeur's eyes widened and he staggered a little on his feet. The next moment he was self-possessed, but the thing had happened. Dawlish was sure that the man had half expected news of this kind.

"An—*ac*cident, sir?"

"And a nasty one. What's your name?"

"Parks, sir."

"Where has Sir Hugo been this morning, Parks?"

"At the office, sir, for the last hour, and before that at home, but——"

"Nowhere else at all?"

"Definitely not, sir; his valet is on holiday, and I have been acting *locum tenens,* sir, but——"

"Take it gently," said Pat Dawlish in a softer voice than usual. "The accident was a fatal one, Parks."

The man was shocked, almost stupefied. His eyes widened and his mouth gaped to show false teeth. He tipped his cap to the back of his head and said: *"Gawd!* Not that!"

"I'm afraid so," said Dawlish, still gently. "Are you quite sure he has only been to the office?"

"Absolutely, sir, but——" Parks was pale and trembling. "I can't understand it, sir, and her leddyship, oh, her leddy-ship . . ."

"Sit down, man," said Dawlish, and he helped Parks to rest on the running board. "Keep your head, and I'll send for a whisky. Cutts, slip along to Pelisse's offices and see whether anyone visited him this morning. Collect names and addresses, and get telephone callers if you can."

"It's a tall order," complained Mr. Cutter gloomily, "but I'll try. You're going to see his wife, I suppose."

"What a brain you've got!" said Dawlish. "Parks, don't move from here, and if a policeman named Trivett should happen to talk to you, tell him Dawlish has gone to Lanster Place."

Parks looked very small and very forlorn, but Dawlish was wondering whether he *had* expected the news of his employer's death. From his first reception of the information, Dawlish was sure of it.

Lanster Place was quite near, and Dawlish reached Pelisse's house within five minutes. Pelisse was such a well-known figure that nine people out of ten could have given his address right away, and could also have made more than a wild guess at his occupation. For Sir Hugo Pelisse was—or had been, Dawlish reminded himself forcefully—the chairman of the National Electrical Council, and as such had lately made something of a stir.

Dawlish did not stop to tell himself that but for Inspector Trivett he would never have suspected Pelisse. He took things as they came, and after ten days of fruitless effort to try to get a line on the Croaker he had gone to the Yard. He had chosen the crucial moment, for if he had delayed the visit, Pelisse's murder would have meant little or nothing to him.

"Good morning, sir," said the man who opened the door of 18 Lanster Place.

"Good morning. Is Lady Pelisse in?"

"She is, sir." The butler, short, rotund, and with an expressionless face, stood aside. Dawlish took a card from his case and waited in the hall while the butler went sedately off.

Dawlish was usually honest with himself and he knew that he was interested in the whole affair, partly because he had been idle for too long and his palmier days on the rugby field were over. It was, however, not at all pleasant to bring the news of a man's death to his wife.

Something clicked in Dawlish's mind.

Lady Pelisse had been a vague thing, simply a name, until that moment. He knew of Pelisse and he knew also that the couple were two of the brightest lights in society, but he was rarely at the functions where they starred, and he had forgotten Lady Pelisse. Now it came to him, forcefully, that he was going to interview La Grana.

La Grana!

He recalled the sensation, when the greatest danseuse in the world—that was claimed and admitted by most people—had left the stage and had married Sir Hugo. La Grana was young, no more than twenty-three, and Pelisse had been nearly fifty. Dawlish had been in France at the time, but the echoes of the affair had reached him.

He had seen her dance a hundred times, and had fallen for the wonderful grace of her smooth limbs, her exquisite body. She was tiny and it was said that she had a temperament.

"If you will come up, sir." The butler had returned, his face expressionless. Dawlish went up the stairs, his blond head showing with sharp relief against the heavy oil paintings of the Pelisse ancestral home. In his silver-gray suit and with his springy stride he seemed out of place.

She was standing by the window of her salon, slim and as lovely as he remembered her. The flowered frock she was wearing might have been molded to her figure from shoulder to waist, but then its lines were flowing. Her eyes, very blue—bluer than even Dawlish's—were deep and luminous, and an absurd thought passed through Pat's mind. Her lips wanted kissing, and he had a sudden vision of Hugo Pelisse's spiky moustache.

"Mr. Dawlish? I don't think we have met for a long time." Her voice was delightful, with only a hint of accent. She was Russian, of course; one of the refugees—no, child of one of the refugees—she was only twenty-six now.

"We haven't," admitted Dawlish, "and I feel I'm not going to be a welcome caller."

"You think not?"

There was something about the way she eyed him that would have excited him a few years before.

"I'm afraid not," said Pat Dawlish. "I'm bringing bad news, Lady Pelisse."

Storm chased the sunshine across that ravishing face.

"Bad *news?*"

Was she naturally as theatrical as this, or was it a pose

which she was making specially for him? And was her frown genuine, or were her eyes laughing while her lips pouted a little and then drew back to reveal a glimpse of her teeth?

"I hardly know why I took it on myself to bring it," said Dawlish, looking somber and very grim. "An accident, Lady Pelisse. A serious one. . . ."

She wasn't acting now. There was a tense, almost animal expression in her eyes.

"My husband?"

"Yes." Dawlish drew a deep breath. "And I'm afraid you will be visited by the police. That's why I came. He was—shot."

"*Shot!*" gasped Lady Pelisse, and her hands went out suddenly and gripped the lapels of Patrick's coat. "Tell me. Did they see who shot him, did they get the man? Tell me!"

7

Who Knew?

A little more than ten minutes before, Pat Dawlish had wondered whether Parks, the chauffeur, had expected the news of Pelisse's murder. Now he was sure that Lady Pelisse had expected it, although her reaction made him stare at her lovely face, twisted now so that it was almost vixenish.

Yes, she had been prepared for the news, either from him or through someone else, and her concern was for the murderer.

"They haven't yet," he said.

Her expression gradually eased, and now grief—or what looked like grief—filled that lovely face. The face of a Delilah, thought Pat Dawlish, who rarely grew dramatic even in his thoughts.

"I—I don't know what to say," she said, and her voice was very soft and gentle. Dawlish could understand the temptation for a man to put his arms around her, for she seemed as if she needed comforting, she looked so forlorn and alone. He coughed, stepped back a pace, and took cigarettes from his pocket. There was a queer, burning sensation at the pit of his stomach.

"Of course not," he said. "It must have been a dreadful shock."

"How can one break bad news?" She smiled at him suddenly, but Dawlish believed her eyes were calculating. She was wondering whether he had noticed the way she had received the news, or whether he believed it was just the effect of the shock. "When—when did it happen?"

Dawlish was glad that she smoked a cigarette with him. She was sitting on a couch now, her hands resting by the sides, their small fingers, with the coral-colored nails, spread out.

He spoke quickly, giving her a résumé of the shooting.

"Had you any idea that this might happen?" he asked.

"None—none at all!" She was suddenly tense, and her expression was almost unpleasant. "Who could have killed Hugo —*Hugo?*"

"Has he seemed worried lately?"

"I have noticed nothing." She took the cigarette from her lips and jumped from the couch. It was easy to understand why she had taken the world by storm, for she moved with a grace that did not seem human. "But I can't stand this, I can't! Where is he, where——?"

Dawlish gripped her forearm. Her flesh was soft and smooth, but her muscles were rigid. Acting, and acting beautifully, he assured himself; he was suddenly convinced that she had wanted her husband dead.

"Easy," he said. "It's the devil, but it can't be helped. What we can do is to find the man who killed him."

Her expression was blank.

"Yes, of course. You know him?"

"I don't, and I don't see how the police can. But you may be able to help."

"I'll do anything—anything!" she assured him, her voice quivering. Yet there could only be one rendering of her first words—she had been *afraid* that the man who had killed Hugo Pelisse had been caught.

"Fine," said Dawlish. "Your husband was here until after eleven, wasn't he?"

"Yes, that's right." She screwed up her face and dabbed at her eyes with a handkerchief, as though to show him she was grieving. "Until half past eleven——"

"He went straight to the office?"

"I—I think so."

"No one came for him here?"

"We had no callers—at least, I was told of none."

"And you've no idea who might have wanted him to die?"

"None—none at all!" cried La Grana. . . . "Who could have killed him? Who——"

She broke off as the telephone bell rang, and Dawlish thought she was glad of the interruption. She took the telephone and said "Hallo" in as cool a voice as he had ever heard, and then she seemed to break down. "Yes, yes, I have heard. It is——"

She replaced the receiver quickly, and Dawlish wondered who had been on the other end of the line. He had no opportunity for finding out, for La Grana took two steps toward him, those wonderful blue eyes rounded; and then suddenly she staggered.

Patrick Dawlish was always a gallant, and he would never have admitted that he disliked the emergency as La Grana fell against him. He was hardly conscious of the fact that she was a woman, but for some queer reason that he could not properly understand he was sure that she was a murderess.

He stopped La Grana from falling and eased her onto the couch. He scowled as he glanced down at her and then, without hesitation, went to the handbag that was lying on the table near the window. There was just a chance that he would learn something from its contents.

He did not know whether he had or not, but he found

enough to make him stare down without moving a muscle. For there was a sheet of paper with several words scrawled on it in pencil, and they read:

I'm going to pay you a visit. The Croaker.

Chief-Inspector William Trivett and Detective-Sergeant Munk had had a busy day. More than a busy day: a harassing one. For there was no clue at all as to the murderer of Sir Hugo Pelisse, but they had learned that he had been shot in the chest.

Dawlish had seen that, and had guessed that the shot had been fired from the dining room, and probably one of its windows. There was a separate entrance into Gay Street from the dining room of the Cranton Club, and a dozen men had passed through it after the shooting. Any one of those dozen men might have shot Pelisse. He had been killed by a slug or bullet from an air rifle, one of the powerful kind that were nearly as dangerous as an ordinary automatic. Killed, in fact, just as Slip Deacon had been killed.

This told Trivett that the two killings had been committed by the Croaker, but at the time Trivett knew nothing of the strange behavior of Lady Naida Pelisse. He was at the Yard at half past six that evening, after interviewing her ladyship and feeling sorry for a puffy-eyed, clinging beauty who seemed to have lost her all now she had lost her husband, when Dawlish appeared in the doorway.

People who had only once visited the Yard before should not have found it possible to get in again without permission, but Dawlish had managed it.

"And I'm big enough to be seen," he assured Trivett. "Well, Bill, how's things?"

"Lousy," admitted William Trivett. "You've heard about the air pistol?"

"Yes, it's in the evening papers. Absolutely clueless otherwise, isn't it?"

"Except the Croaker clue," said Trivett. "It was a Croaker murder, Dawlish, and the Croaker *was* connected with Pelisse."

"What made you think so in the first place?"

Trivett frowned, wondering if it was wise to give Dawlish the information. On the other hand, the story would probably be in the press within a couple of days, and it could not do much damage. In any case, it was preposterous to suspect Dawlish of being connected with the Croaker.

"We picked up a fence the other day who has been handling a lot of stuff for the Croaker. He told us that he had first contacted with the Croaker at the Greet Club. So we grew interested in the Greet Club and learned the members of the syndicate backing it. Now, that syndicate," went on Trivett, "must be worth five or six million pounds. Faversham and Fayre are both millionaires and Pelisse must have been close. A queer syndicate to be running a gaming club. Reputations to break, money to lose—the whole thing looked a cloak."

"For the Croaker."

"Yes." Trivett scratched his ear. "The same syndicate seemed too big to worry about the Croaker, unless the Croaker is one of them."

"I think we can say it wasn't Pelisse," said Dawlish. "How much has the Croaker got away with in the past year?"

"Three or four hundred thousand pounds' worth of stuff, one way and another. He uses a thief once and no more. In effect it's a racket," added Trivett, with a rueful smile. "The crooks can generally do what they want, but each has to give up the proceeds of one night's work to the Croaker. The Croaker plans the raid, works everything out, and sends the man—as he sent Slip Deacon—to the job. If the police get going, the Croaker's just a name, and the unfortunate crook gets the sentence. Of course, the Towers' affair was a little different, but it was the same in the main principles."

Dawlish nodded, and slumped over a chair. Sergeant Munk, whose florid face was paler than usual because he was hungry and thirsty, thought he looked a fool. Other people often thought that of Patrick Dawlish.

"Why did the Croaker bump Pelisse off, if he did?" Dawlish asked.

"*If* he did," said Trivett. "Of course he did, and I'd say it was because Pelisse was threatening to cause trouble."

"A nice watertight reasoning," smiled Dawlish, and for some reason Munk revised his opinion. "Look here, I'm going to pay back what you've paid me. You put me onto Pelisse and I'll square the account, but after this I'm working on my own."

Trivett laughed.

"Don't expect us to rescue you, and remember the Croaker's a killer."

Patrick Dawlish stood up, a picture of affronted dignity.

"You'll rue that, Bill! Listen. Lady La Grana Pelisse was pleased her husband was killed. She was worried about the possibility of you finding the murderer. She hoodwinked you, I don't doubt, but it's a fact. So it *might* have been the *crime passionelle,* the air gun might have been a coincidence; Pelisse might have had nothing to do with the Croaker, and if I were you I'd watch his widow's boyfriends. So long."

Chief-Inspector William Trivett looked at the closed door with an expression on his face that even puzzled Munk. Then he stood up, slowly and deliberately, and walked to the door.

"Dawlish is beginning to worry me. Either he knows more than he should—that is, he knows the Croaker—or he thinks he's clever. If he really does ‾get on the Croaker's trail, he'll be dead in a week. Money on it, Munk?"

Sergeant Albert Munk wrinkled his red nose, grunted, put his hand in his pocket, and brought out four half-crowns.

"Money on it," he said. "If Dawlish gets on the Croaker, it's the Croaker's good-bye. I like that man. How did *you* find Mrs. Pelisse? Hysterical, eh? Wool-over-the-eyes, eh?"

"Lady Pelisse," corrected Trivett, ignoring the question. "Munk, we'll have someone watching the Greet Club tonight after all."

8

The Greet Club

The murder of Sir Hugo Pelisse created sensation enough to squeeze everything else from the front pages of the evening papers. Pelisse himself had been a big figure in the national financial world. His murder put him on the front page, and the shooting at London's most exclusive club put the finishing touch to an editor's dream.

At seven-thirty that evening, over a comfortable meal paid for by Dawlish and supplied by Fortnum & Mason—Dawlish had a service flat and lacked a man—Messrs. Dawlish, Beresford, Cutter, and Rawling read their several papers, made their various comments, and drank excellent wines. Dawlish finished first.

Beresford's bull-like face moved from his paper.

"Happy now?"

"I'm reasonably happy, although I wasn't until I squeezed out of La Grana's salon, and it's a good thing you weren't there, lady-killer. Question—did the Croaker kill Pelisse, or was it Grana's lover?"

"Your mind runs that way," said Beresford. "Pat, you asked us ten days ago whether we would like to join you in a manhunt. We've drunk half the East End pubs dry, and now——"

"Pelisse did die," broke in the dirgelike Cutter, "and that proves it isn't all a lie. The *Star*'s mentioned the Croaker, too. Any of the others?"

49

Beresford and Rawling, reading different papers, shook their heads. Dawlish poured out more claret.

"Joking apart," he said, "this is getting nasty. The murder of Pelisse makes it front-page news, and the affair will come before the gentlemen of Westminster before we're much older. I'm wagering that the Croaker's preparing for his swan song or—mark you—for bigger things than he's done before. I mean he's stirred real mud this time."

"He must have known what would happen," growled Cutter. Cutter had a very sharp face, which suggested that his parents had been well named, and he was nearly bald. What hair he still possessed was spread to its uttermost across his head, but he looked a man nearer sixty than thirty from an aerial view. He had passed his amateur lightweight degrees with honors, and continued to surprise strangers with his deep voice.

"Fool if he didn't," said Beresford.

Mr. Dawlish regarded the fourth member of the party and requested his opinion. The opinion of Tony Rawling was usually worth having, because it was rarely expressed. He was a man who either had no ideas or kept them to himself, and his favorite sport was fishing. Among other things he inclined— he said—to corpulence, but most folks called him fat.

"Plenty of other places to kill a man," he remarked. Dawlish's blue eyes gleamed.

"Gad, you've got it! He was killed there deliberately——"

"To create a sensation," snapped Beresford.

"To get the Croaker in the news," growled Cutter.

"Damned good advertising," said Dawlish, with an odd expression in his eyes. "Now I wonder whether Trivett or the Yard has made the same discovery," said Dawlish. "There are two things I want to do. Visit the Greet Club, and see what the other four members of the syndicate are feeling like tonight."

"Meaning Faversham, Fayre, Renway, and Golding," said

Beresford, rubbing his cheeks. "They were all at the Cranton this morning, Pat, you knew that?"

Dawlish, who had been busy in so many ways, glared.

"What am I supposed to have—eyes in my rear? I didn't know, and for the love of Mike don't hide up facts like that, Ted; they might be important. So all four of them were there?"

"First time Golding's ever been in the place," contributed Cutter. "He's not a member. The others are."

Dawlish lit a cigarette.

"So-ho, we're getting on. It was a meeting between the five of them, and the Croaker didn't want Pelisse to see the others. That might even squash your reasoning, Tony. Pelisse might have been killed in the sensational circumstances because there had not been a chance to get him anywhere else. Anyhow, there are the two possibilities. That they killed Pelisse to stop him talking to the others, or just to stop him talking. What time does the Greet Club open?"

"Seven," said Cutter. "They do dinners downstairs."

"Two millionaires and two M.P.'s running a restaurant, eh? I think, for the purpose of the evening, it will be as well if we all go. Without any ladies. Tony, you take Ted. Cutts, I'll take you, and remember it's on business."

Mr. Cornelius Greet, the manager and ostensibly the owner of the Greet Club, was a man who fitted his part to perfection. He was tall, middle-aged, with a presence and a forefront, a man who possessed the most perfect manners imaginable and with a soft, modulated voice and a delightful smile. In a dark way he was handsome, but it was obvious he was not English. He was, in fact, a Greek.

He was his usual smiling self as he greeted the members of the club that evening. There were, as Cutter had said, facilities for dining on the first floor of the house, but few people took advantage of it. The chief attraction of the club was the gaming tables, and after eight o'clock the rooms began to fill up. Usually by ten o'clock they were comfortably full, and by midnight they were overcrowded.

Fewer clients than usual were present when the party from Dawlish's flat made its entrance, and it was rather unkind of the only woman there who was young and attractive to bump into Beresford. Beresford sometimes claimed, modestly, that he just stood and smiled and they swarmed round him.

The girl was little more than twenty, dressed in a dark red gown that was modest for the period, and her dark hair was piled above her head. The tiara in her hair looked worth a fortune, and somehow helped to create the illusion that she was foreign. She apologized gracefully, and Beresford liked her voice.

"I'm so sorry. No damage?"

"I'm not hurt," smiled Beresford. He took the girl's arm and walked toward a couch in one corner of the room. "You're not a regular visitor, are you?"

"If I was, wouldn't you have recognized me?"

"Yes, I would. Like a drink?"

"Not yet, but I'm a little nervous." She looked anything but shy, and Beresford told himself that she could have found the nerve for anything; her eyes were gray and, he thought, daring.

"I can't believe it," he said. "But let's get to a table. Roulette?"

"I've been brought up on it."

"Don't stake too high," he said protectively; "it's surprising how money goes."

"I've plenty," said the girl in red, and when her laugh came it was low-pitched and delightful. "Do you always take a fatherly interest before you're introduced?"

"And after," said Beresford. "Beresford, called Ted. You?"

"Fayre, called Joan," said the lady in red, and Beresford had a shock.

Fayre—daughter, of course, of Horatio Fayre, one of the syndicate of five!

He covered his surprise well, and they found a place at a table. Joan Fayre's father was a millionaire, and she did her best to prove it, for she lost a small fortune in the next hour, while Beresford was trying to think straight. It was fantastic to believe that Fayre, if he helped to run this place for profit, would allow his daughter to play such high stakes. Not that Joan Fayre looked as though she was likely to wait for permission from anyone.

Beresford was quietening his conscience and pointing out to himself that he had a good excuse for his gallantry that night ready for when he banged into Dawlish. It was a fact that he could never resist a pretty face. As the evening wore on he saw that she was becoming fascinated by the game. The spinning wheel, the drone of the croupier's voice, the sliding of the checks, everything seemed to get in her blood, and her eyes were like gray pools of fire.

Dawlish and Cutter were at another table. Dawlish had played a little, and as luck would have it he had won three times running. He called it his limit, and looked about him.

Fifty or sixty people were in the room, and most were men. Of the women, twelve were of the dowager type who found a synthetic amusement in gambling. The others were with men, except Joan Fayre.

Dawlish had learned Joan's name and was satisfied that Ted's lure of the ladies was proving useful.

Dawlish felt Cutts jerk his arm and looked up. As he did so he saw the reason, and his lips tightened. For Horatio Fayre—who had made his money out of South American cattle deals—had entered the room, and was standing by the door.

A short, corpulent man with a heavy white moustache, he looked something like a nonconformist parson or lay preacher. Even in his immaculate evening dress he seemed out of place. He was smiling, and his rosy cheeks were shining, until he saw Joan.

Dawlish saw the frown and the expression in his eyes, and watched covertly but carefully. Fayre went to a waiter and sent a message to Joan. Dawlish saw the girl look up, frown, and mutter something to Ted Beresford. Then she approached her father, and she looked gay and cheerful against the man's grimness.

"Fayre doesn't approve, so he probably *is* in the ramp," muttered Dawlish. "Hallo, Ted, being useful for once?"

"She's not exactly on the best of terms with Papa," vouchsafed Beresford, looming up beside Dawlish and Cutter. "Her comment on him was almost low, Pat. Have you seen Faversham?"

Dawlish nodded slowly.

"Faversham, Golding, and Renway—the whole syndicate's here now that Fayre's arrived. And they're all looking cheerful, except Fayre."

"Ye-es," said Beresford. "Do you know, Pat, I don't think we'll get much tonight, but if we follow Pelisse's four friends home we might learn a bit. I—— Gawd!"

He drawled the word out deliberately, and there was an echo of it in the other's minds. For the door had opened again. This time to admit a woman and a man. The man meant nothing; none of the four men from the flat recognized him; but all of them saw La Grana—or the Lady (Naida) Pelisse.

She was here, after what had happened that morning!

The silence that followed her entry was complete. Everyone in the room was surprised or shocked, but La Grana seemed to notice nothing.

"A full house, Percy, after all."

Percy's high-pitched voice, almost a falsetto, came quickly; but what he said was lost in the general hum of conversation. Everyone present was aware that he—or she—had dropped a brick.

It seemed to prove that the grief she had shown to the police —and had tried to show to him—had been synthetic. It would be impossible for any woman to be here within twelve hours of her husband's death, if she were really heartbroken.

Dawlish looked at the man accompanying her. The man she called Percy.

He was tall and spindly, perhaps the most ungainly man present, and he was certainly no fit companion for a woman of La Grana's beauty. He was sandy and very fair, and his watery blue eyes were covered by a pair of rimless but gold-fitted spectacles. "Percy" suited him well.

Dawlish ticked Percy off in his mind as a man to watch, for he looked weak and likely to talk. He agreed with Beresford that nothing was likely to happen that night, and he almost wondered whether it was worth waiting to follow the four members of the syndicate reputed to be backing Greet's. Faversham and the others were all playing, and all looking serious. Greet walked from table to table, smooth-voiced and soft-footed. The hum of conversation kept at the same monotonous level, although from a small anteroom came the occasional clink of a glass and a woman's voice raised in laughter. The croupiers were droning, the rakes clinking on the counters. The smoke was filtering upward toward the soft white lights. It might have been Monaco. . . .

And then came a shout, a scream, and a high-pitched cry: *"Police!"*

9

Mr. Dawlish Acts

The cry was so sudden and unexpected that it worked like a spell, and kept every man and woman at the club motionless. Dawlish was reminded vividly of the affair at the Cranton that morning when Pelisse had died. He mentally photographed Fayre, looking like a frightened rabbit, Sir Charles Faversham, tall and distinguished and fitting his name, staring open-mouthed toward the door, Joan Fayre with her hands at her throat, next to her father, Lady Pelisse staring at the weedy Percy as though in supplication, and Greet standing like a graven image with fear on his smooth face.

Once again Dawlish moved first and spoke first.

"Police, is it, friends? Is there a way out, Greet?"

"I—I——" started Greet; but before he could go any farther the door was pushed open and the men in blue appeared.

Dawlish was smiling now, and looking cheerful. Beresford said something under his breath and Tony Rawling said, distinctly, that it was a fair cop.

A dozen people were moving, but they were like sheep without a leader. Three men seemed more in control of themselves than anyone else, and Dawlish moved toward these, with his three friends bringing up the rear.

A big, burly man in blue, with a sergeant's stripes, shot out a hand and gripped Dawlish.

"Stop just where you are, please."

"The 'please' saved you," murmured Dawlish, and he stopped. "Ted, be ready for a mill. Sergeant, go and kiss Auntie for a minute. What made you raid us tonight?"

"Information about drugs," said the burly sergeant. He had apparently decided that there was nothing to fear from the blond man, and he went with every evidence of satisfaction toward the tables. By the croupiers were the chips, but at the chemin-de-fer and the baccarat tables the money was there, in anything from fivers to hundred-pound notes. In one corner a small-change and cash desk was fitted with a safe; five men in blue were near it.

Still Greet seemed struck dumb, but two women were moaning, and Joan Fayre was looking tight-lipped toward her father.

Seven uniformed men were in the room now, and two plainclothes men were busy counting the money at the desk, and searching the safe. One of the earlier players—apparently a stool pigeon—was talking cheerfully to them, and Cutter's deep voice came:

"The louse. I'll crown him one day. Going to make a break for it?"

"Patience," said Dawlish. "I want to see how they play."

The guests of the Greet Club were being lined up against the wall, and Dawlish watched their reactions. One or two men protested, but most did as they were told. The whole crowd was ready at last with the exception of Dawlish, his three friends, and their three allies, who were grouped together farthest away from the door.

One plainclothes man and a sergeant started to walk the line, taking down names and address. At least five men out of the first dozen were liars, and three gave the name of Smith. Dawlish was thinking fast, telling himself that it was almost incredible that there was no second exit, that if there wasn't, the proprietors of the gaming house were either fools or criminals, for they must have known the possibility of a raid. But he was thinking also of other things.

Ted Beresford was fidgeting.

"If we're going to mix it, mix it."

"Patience—Joan's all right, the Pa's there. Twelve men in blue and three in plainclothes—that's two apiece. You three are willing?"

He was talking *sotto voce,* ignoring the glare of the red-faced sergeant, who looked as though he wanted to split up the group. He didn't try, and the three gamblers who looked ready for trouble nodded or grunted.

"I'm warning you," muttered Dawlish, "there might be shooting."

"Don't be a——" began Ted Beresford, and then his homely face showed outraged understanding. "*Pat,* you don't think——"

"That's just what I do think. There isn't a genuine police-man in the bunch, and I ought to know. They're the Croaker's men."

Beresford looked as though he had swallowed a caramel whole, Tony Rawling gulped, Cutter just growled. The three likely looking men hesitated, and Dawlish told himself he could rely on them at a pinch. And the pinch was coming, for these men in blue looked beautiful, but the raid was a fraud, the whole thing was a hoax. He believed he knew why Pelisse had been killed now, and he was raging. But outwardly he was wearing that inane smile. Then his hand hit his pocket and came away with a gun.

"Back there! Hands on your heads."

There was a split second of silence, and then a woman's scream. As the scream came, one of the plainclothes men pulled a gun, and fired a fraction of a second later than Dawlish. Two stabs of flame, two sharp *hisses,* two bullets honing across the room, and two dull *plops.* Something seemed to snatch at Dawlish's coat sleeve, but the other gunman staggered backward.

The room was in uproar. A dozen men sprang forward desperately toward the door, but as they crowded there the men in blue drew guns. Dawlish leapt, with the others, for the nearest table and crouched behind it. Beresford, Cutts, and Rawling had guns and used them. Flames were spitting, bullets striking, now and again a man's curse split the air. Smoke was curling upward and the gamblers were crowding back against the walls, while the pseudo-policemen were behind another table, returning the blond man's fire.

It was a holocaust.

Beresford took a bullet in the shoulder and swore; Dawlish picked off the red-faced sergeant and saw him fall, but this was worse than he had expected. His chief thought as he hid his head and fired, was whether the Croaker was there.

Then the second interruption came, an incredible thing but a genuine one this time. Footsteps pounded on the stairs outside, two pseudo-policemen almost fell into the room, and one man's cry came clearly.

"The cops, the cops!"

"The real ones," muttered Dawlish. "We've got the swine!"

But he was wrong.

The firing stopped on the instant, and Dawlish hadn't the heart to fire at sitting men. Then Cornelius Greet moved, sweating now and no longer suave, toward the cash desk. He reached it, passed it, and in the wall by its side a gaping hole appeared.

Dawlish swore and leapt forward, but he had no chance to succeed. Something hit him on the side of the head and he went down. Even as he was falling he saw the men in blue crowding toward the opening, two men with guns holding the others off. Then suddenly the panel in the wall slid to, and a queer silence reigned. Then the real police came, with the bucolic Sergeant Munk in the lead, and Chief-Inspector Trivett close behind.

"What's the damage?" asked Pat Dawlish. "I know my head is aching but I can stand that."

Trivett, looking very cold and grim, grunted.

"We've got three of the Croaker's men again—you like the number three, don't you? Three others are hurt, and a woman. Greet's gone, and I think some of the gamblers got away. Did you recognize anyone tonight?"

"Only Lady Pelisse," Dawlish said.

"*She* was here, was she?" Trivett was too surprised by the news to realize the possibility that Dawlish wasn't telling the whole truth.

They were in the anteroom, and the others had gone home. The police were in complete control.

The blackjack that had sent Dawlish down had struck only a glancing blow. He had seen Faversham and Fayre, with the other two members of the syndicate, Lady Pelisse and Percy, Joan Fayre, and one or two others following the pseudo-policeman through the hole in the wall, and he could not blame any of them.

Trivett rubbed his cheek.

"I would never have believed she would have had the nerve. I had a man watching her, too. Can you think of another name for the Croaker, Dawlish?"

"Poacher. I'd already thought of it," said Dawlish, whose head was aching. "Another show like the Towers. A nice wealthy gathering, a room lousy with money, a police raid that looked genuine, and a complete cleanout. I should say Pelisse obviously knew what was planned, and was going to warn the others. That's why they killed him."

"Looks like it," admitted Inspector Trivett.

"Who started the roughhouse?"

"I did, with my little gun. I've a license for it. The others showed guns too, but didn't feel like mass murder. Any of your prisoners likely to talk?"

"I don't think they know anything," said Trivett. "Have a look at them, will you, in case you've seen any of them before."

"Where are they?"

"Downstairs in the dining room; you haven't far to go."

Dawlish followed Trivett and Munk downstairs, and interviewed the three men he—or his friends—had shot. Dawlish knew none of them.

"If we could have got Greet it would have helped. You'll have a call out for him?"

"It's out. And we're watching the syndicate."

They went downstairs. Inside it had been hot, and the crisp December air was welcome. It seemed to clear Dawlish's head.

"What did you get out of the three?"

"The usual story," said Trivett. "They're all well-known racecourse gangsters. The Poacher sent for them this morning, and they dared not refuse to obey him."

"Terrorism to a fine art. I wonder if he'll stop at the East End."

"You mean the Croaker?"

"Oh no," said Pat Dawlish genially, "I mean the man in the moon. I'm going, Bill, and I might be at my flat if you want me. Remember to have La Grana watched very carefully, won't you?"

Trivett said somewhat heavily that he would, and went back

to the Yard in a police car to receive congratulations at having men near the Greet Club. The morning's papers would give him more than a little praise, although he knew that but for Dawlish he would have done nothing and heard nothing. Munk looked like winning his money.

Patrick Dawlish and Edward Beresford, meanwhile, made their way to Dawlish's Clarge Street flat, reasonably well pleased. Rawling and Cutter had gone on a mission of inquiry, and were due at the flat at midnight. Dawlish knew there would be beer waiting, and he was looking forward to it.

He might have looked forward to meeting the two gentlemen at that moment sitting in his flat and drinking his beer had he known of their presence, but he had no idea they were there. But they guessed he was coming, and they had their guns very handy. Unlike the three prisoners, they were the Croaker's regular men and knew their business.

For the Croaker had decided that Mr. Dawlish had gone too far.

10

Lost Cause?

Dawlish was thoughtful as he approached Clarge Street, which explained why he had elected to walk. Beresford was asking himself whether, in a fair and unbiased competition, her eyes or her ankles would win. Probably both. Joan Fayre had been very lovely, and he refused to believe that she knew anything about her father's possibly nefarious practices.

Dawlish was thinking of the East End of London.

The man who had introduced him to this business had come from the East End of London. Slip Deacon, in short. So had the three men who had masqueraded as policemen. So had the three men now in prison, after the attempt on the vault at Rendle Towers.

The Croaker certainly took most of his men from the East.

Dawlish had come to that conclusion before, and he had worked the pubs of the neighborhood between Aldgate and the three-mile limit. But whenever he had mentioned the Croaker, a pall had fallen over the gathering, and even free beer had loosened no tongues.

Dawlish was thinking that it was time he looked down East again.

The question was, should he start that night or wait until morning?

He decided to wait until morning, and told Beresford what

he had decided. Beresford said her hair was black, not red, and apologized. Dawlish inserted the key in the hole and turned the handle quickly, by habit.

It was the gunman's misfortune that he was standing close to the door and the wood smote him. Dawlish saw the door swinging back, heard the man's gasp, and dropped without a second's hesitation to his knees. His gun was in his hand in a flash and his voice was like a rasp.

"Drop 'em. Both of you!"

He touched the trigger of his gun, aiming at a wisp of hair, and almost scalped his man. Two shots came at him and missed him by a fraction. If he darted back he would still be vulnerable.

He went forward like a bull, roaring all the time. Beresford saw him leaping toward the chair which was sheltering one man, kicking a beer bottle as he went. The beer smashed against the wall and the bottle broke with a crash, while a bullet tore the end of Dawlish's trousers. But as he went he overturned the chair, sending its full weight on the gunman.

Dawlish twisted on his feet and saw the second man, dark-faced, standing by the door and firing. He didn't know how he missed being hit until he realized the man was shooting left-handed—his right hand was hanging limply at his side. The result of the door crashing against him. Dawlish touched his own trigger. The gun clattered from the other's grasp, and Dawlish stopped. He had a habit of looking as though he was out for a stroll, no matter what the circumstances.

"Hurt, sonny? All right, Ted."

"You," admitted Mr. Beresford, entering, "take the biscuit. I'll admit it. That made me sweat." He stooped down and helped himself to the gunman's automatic—his own was empty, which explained his reticence—and stepped to the man who had been crushed by the chair. The leg had caught him behind the ear, and sent him to a long sleep. Beresford said as much, and Dawlish, eyeing the other man genially, nodded.

"That'll do me. Phone for Trivett, will you?"

"Whitehall one-two-one-two?"

"Yes, that's the number." Dawlish's blue eyes, very bright, were fixed on the wounded gunman's. Beresford had the receiver off the telephone and was dialing when the man took a step forward.

"No—*don't!*"

"Don't what?" asked Dawlish genially.

"Send for the police—don't, I tell you! I'll do anything—anything——"

"Just what is meant by 'anything'?" asked Pat Dawlish, motioning Beresford. "The name of the Croaker, for instance?"

"I don't know it, I swear I don't, but . . . I daren't face the police."

"That suggests you've a black past," said Dawlish conversationally. "What's your name?"

"Brenner."

"Address?"

"Ten Melfer Street, Shoreditch, but——"

"A regular gunman for the Croaker?"

The man hesitated. Dawlish studied him, seeing the rather beetling forehead, the shifty eyes, the slack mouth which revealed two stumps of teeth, although the others were fine and white. He could see the man trembling.

"Y-yes, I work for the Croaker. But the police——"

"You probably won't understand what a square deal is," said Dawlish easily. "But if you come clean I won't send you to the police. Your name is Brenner, and you live at ten Melfer Street, Shoreditch. You work regularly for the Croaker. You get your orders by——"

"Messenger."

"His name?"

"I don't know."

"You've a meeting place?"

Brenner's slack mouth tightened for a moment, and then he nodded, his eyes moving to and fro as though in search of succor.

"Yes—the Magpie—Aldgate High Street. We meet twice a week regularly, but the Croaker's not there. Morelli is. Morelli is——"

"Who is Morelli?" asked Dawlish slowly. He believed that the man was telling the truth, but he also proposed to make sure of it before he let the man go. It might take a few days, but that didn't matter.

"Mor—Morelli's the Speaker. I——"

"Speaks for the Croaker, does he. That sounds almost like the Houses of Parliament, doesn't it? When does the messenger call?"

"Usually at midday."

"Does he always speak personally?"

"If I'm out he sends a message—leaves a note for me."

"Where have you got to report tonight?"

"To—to the Speaker!"

"At the Magpie?"

"Yes, by the telephone."

Dawlish hitched up his trousers, for this was getting better every moment.

"And the code word is?"

"Just—just ask for the Speaker. Then say: Number Seventeen. He'll ask questions."

"And how do you answer?"

"The fewest words possible. But, Dawlish, if the Croaker thought——"

"The Croaker can look after himself and I can look after

66

you," said Dawlish cheerfully. "There's nothing else that might trip me up?"

"No, no, nothing at all!"

"No one watching outside?"

"Nothing, I tell you! Dawlish, the police——"

"I'm not going to turn you over to them and I'm not going to let you go," said Dawlish gently. "You're going to have a holiday, and if you haven't told the truth, God help you. Ted, get my revered Uncle Jeremy on the line, will you?"

"Confounded impertinence!" growled Sir Jeremy Pinkerton ten minutes or so later. "I won't do it. Finally no, no, NO! Is that clear? Why, you pernickety fool, do you think I want to play with a gun at my age? I was seventy-one last week and——"

"The top floor will do nicely," said Dawlish, "and Ted Beresford will bring them; I just want you to look after them for a few days. Only the two, and be careful they don't bite. No, there's no need for a doctor."

"You . . ." said Sir Jeremy, and then his voice quavered upward in a cackle. "What time have I got to wait up till?"

"Ted'll arrive with the prisoners about three," promised Dawlish. "Keep Parsons up, but no one else. The top floor isn't used these days, is it, except by Parsons?"

Sir Jeremy admitted that only his butler used the top floor of the Towers, and hung up.

Dawlish and Beresford tied the prisoner's wrists and ankles —the unconscious man would come around soon and he was badly hurt—and used sticking plaster as a gag. By the time he had finished, Rawling and Cutter arrived, and commented strongly.

"Keep the party clean," protested Dawlish. "Tony, you're going down to Surrey with Ted. The uncle has offered to look

67

after these birds temporarily. Cutts, how many of your friends stay awake all night?"

"A hundred and seventeen," said Cutts. "Who pinched the beer?"

"Never mind the beer. Get seven of them, and tell them to locate the Magpie in the Aldgate High Street. Just locate it and nose around."

"The gymnasium's shut at one o'clock," complained Cutts. "What's on?"

"I don't exactly know," admitted Dawlish, "but I want to talk to the Speaker, and I want anyone who comes out of the Magpie followed after I've phoned. Several might come out. Tell your friends to be careful, because I believe one of the others has a gun."

Cutts rubbed his thin nose and glowered.

"Come clean," he said.

Dawlish explained briefly.

There had been a time when Cutter had specialized in the fistic art, and in that time he had met a great many people politely called pugilists. Some, oddly enough, were fond of Mr. Cutter. They were members of an East End gymnasium, and he could call on them when he liked. Dawlish saw a way of using them that night. He wanted the Magpie watched, but did not want the police there.

Cutter went off for his men blithely, for he saw the chance of a scrap. Beresford's car—or Beresford *père's* car—a Daimler of large proportions, was pressed into service, and Beresford drove himself, Rawling, and the two unfortunate Croaker's men to the home of Sir Jeremy Pinkerton, for safe custody. And Pat Dawlish, his heart beating faster perhaps than it should have done, hurried to Piccadilly, found a late cab, and drove to Melfer Street, Shoreditch.

There was a telephone kiosk at the corner of the road, and

after sending the cabbie to the High Street to wait for further orders, he used it.

The hoarse voice of a man at the Magpie answered him, and Dawlish asked gruffly for the Speaker. Then he waited, and all the time he was imagining the voices of the men who had played any part in the affair at the Greet Club, or . . .

And then he had a shock, for the Speaker came on the line; and the Speaker's voice was very soft and pleasing. It was a woman's.

11

The Speaker

The chance that this was a wrong number flashed through Dawlish's mind, but the man's harsh voice had already admitted it to be the Magpie. And Dawlish had asked for the Speaker.

Was the Speaker always a woman? Was this Morelli? Dawlish told himself that the man Brenner had been talking about a member of the male species, not of a woman. So he chanced his arm.

"Who is that?"

The voice at the other end of the line broke into a laugh. Dawlish made peculiar faces at the glass of the kiosk. He might have been talking to a girl who could keep her head—to Delia, for instance, or Joan Fayre, or even to La Grana, but certainly not to a member of the Croaker's organization.

He was trying to place the voice, but he could not, although he was reasonably sure that it was not La Grana's. That left Joan Fayre as a possibility. . . .

The woman stopped laughing, and there was a note of seriousness in her voice.

"Of course, you didn't expect me tonight. Who is that?"

"Number Seventeen," said Dawlish keeping his voice as gruff as possible, and feeling his heart hammering against his ribs.

"Seven-*teen*!" It was an exclamation, and Dawlish wondered what the woman's face was like. "Yes, of course. Well?"

"It's finished," said Dawlish.

There was a pause this time, and he distinctly heard a gulp at the other end of the wire. Then came the woman's voice, hard and flat—and astonishingly like La Grana's when she had wanted to know whether her husband's murderer had been found.

"I see. You are sure?"

"Yes. There were two of them."

"Very—good," said the woman who was called the Speaker. "That is all right, Seventeen. A message will be delivered, tomorrow, as usual. Good night."

"G'night." Dawlish waited until the telephone at the other end had been replaced. Then he stepped from the kiosk and wiped the sweat from his forehead.

He had expected to hear the voice of a man, a note of something sinister, a grimness that would be part and parcel of the campaign of the Croaker. Instead he had talked to a girl who might have been flirting with a would-be philanderer on the telephone. That note of gaiety at the beginning of the conversation stuck in his mind.

The cabbie drove to Mile End Road station, after telling Dawlish that the Magpie was a hundred yards farther down the road, and Dawlish walked quickly toward the pub. He passed a policeman, who touched his helmet and wished him good night while wondering what the young gent was doing in that part of the world at that time of night. As he neared the Magpie, Dawlish crossed to the other side of the road and turned up the collar of his mackintosh. He had no desire to be seen by anyone who might recognize him.

The Magpie was a bigger building than Dawlish had expected, built on a corner and having a fine view of the crossroads. There were dozens of signs declaring this or that beer was sold, and others claiming the Magpie's luncheons were easily the best in the Mile End Road. It looked, in fact, like a perfectly genuine business house where the service would be good and the food more than edible.

He went past without appearing to look right or left. Directly opposite the Magpie a man stood in the corner of a millinery shop doorway. Three doors along another shroudy figure was waiting. Dawlish whistled three times, loudly enough for the sound to echo across the road.

From the opposite pavement a man loomed from the shadows and walked rapidly toward Dawlish. He did not stop to talk, but he showed his face for a fraction of a second; it was Cutts. Dawlish chuckled to himself for Cutts was playing this game very well indeed. He knew that there was a chance that someone would be watching from the Magpie, and he had no desire to let it be thought that he was meeting anyone by appointment.

Dawlish followed the bald-headed boxer to the first turning, and found Cutter waiting.

"Any luck, Pat?"

"The Speaker tonight was a woman, which suggests it's a changing office," said Dawlish. "You?"

"Two men left ten minutes ago. How long since you phoned?"

"Twenty minutes. Were they followed?"

"Yes, and they'll be traced, don't worry about that."

"Sure no woman came out?"

"I'm sure."

"Any of your friends object to a bit of burglary?"

"You'll have to pay them well," said Cutts.

"Offer them fifty apiece," said Dawlish. Cutter hurried off, and the five remaining members of the pugilistic profession agreed, for the consideration of fifty pounds apiece, to burgle the Magpie.

Dawlish had not been consciously aware of the fact that he proposed to enter the place, but it had been at the back of his mind from the moment Brenner had talked. He was longing to start an offensive, for he had been on the defense too long.

How Cutter and the five men managed to keep hidden as a policeman passed on his rounds Dawlish didn't know; and he did not inquire, for some things could best remain mysteries. The steady plop-plop of the man's footsteps echoed for a time, until they died in the silence, and then Cutter materialized out of the darkness again.

"All set, Pat?"

"Fine. Back door, I take it?"

"Yes, there's an alleyway. Leave two men by the front, shall we, to keep a watch?"

"That's an idea," agreed Dawlish.

They went forward toward the rear of the Magpie. Dawlish knew how to move quietly, and even in those London streets he managed to merge with the shadows. Cutter was just behind him, and when they reached the alley they saw the three toughs, hefty-looking fellows dressed in mackintoshes and cloth caps, waiting nearby.

Dawlish slipped into the lead. His eyes were gleaming and his heart banging against his ribs, for this was the first time he had tried anything quite like it.

He stopped smiling as he examined the small door that led to the courtyard at the back of the Magpie.

"It's easy," he said. "I'll hop over and open it. Keep together until we're at the house, and then spread out. I'm going in first."

"The house door'll be locked," said Cutter.

"I've met locks and locks," said Dawlish. "Is there an expert here in case of difficulty?"

A gentleman whom Cutter addressed as Willie volunteered the information that he could do most things with locks, although he had been out of the profession for a long time.

The rear door of the Magpie proved a tough proposition. So tough that the expert elected to try one of the windows. After a few seconds the catch was slipped back and the window pulled up.

Dawlish was on the tiptoe of excitement, but no sound came, although he had been prepared for a tremendous clangor when the window had gone up. The people of the Magpie apparently cared nothing for burglar alarms. If this place *was* the headquarters of the Croaker's organization, that wasn't hard to explain. Few people in that part of London would have thought of burgling the Croaker.

It was pitch dark inside, for the lights from the streetlamps were cut off by the high wall that surrounded the premises. Dawlish, his smile there as always and his hands very steady, entered the scullery and found the door leading to the kitchen. Not until then did he use the torch that he had in his hand.

The little circle of light shone on the kitchen door, and Dawlish found and turned the handle. The silence was absolute, and but for the fact that he knew there were men behind him would have believed himself alone.

The kitchen door was not locked, and he found himself at the threshold of a long, narrow passage. Somehow he had not expected it, but he went forward, still without making a sound, to find that there were no doors along it for at least twelve feet. That meant if they left a man by the kitchen door their way of retreat could not be cut off.

"Useful," he said gently through the darkness, and his whisper seemed to float about him.

"Useful," he repeated, for there had been no answer. There was still no answer, and Pat Dawlish swung round on his heel, with a muttered imprecation on his lips. But it was cut short, and he stood there staring—at nothing.

Nothing! The passage and the kitchen were empty; there was no sign of Cutter or the three men with him. But they had been there thirty seconds before.

12

Surprise Packet

Dawlish stood where he was, halfway along the passage and peering toward the door through which he had just entered, hardly daring to breathe and feeling a cold, clammy sensation at his spine and the pit of his stomach.

He had had many surprises in the past few days and as many shocks, but nothing as uncanny as this. He moved neither backward nor forward, but stood with a torch in his hand. And then someone swore, and he changed the torch over and grabbed at his gun.

It was in his pocket, very comforting. No sound came now that the echoes of his single exclamation had died away, and there was still no sign of the others. A sweat of perspiration burst over his face, and he wiped his cheeks.

He reached the kitchen and the scullery again. Both were empty. At the bottom of the courtyard he could see the gate swinging open—the gate he had opened. But no one was there.

Dawlish wiped his neck again, and looked back. Everything was in darkness inside the house. Cutter and three other men had vanished.

Dawlish had to decide whether to go back or go forward, and he disliked the idea of retreating. Among other things there was the fact that *if* something inexplicable had happened, Cutter and the bruisers were in Queen Street, and they would need his help.

He turned from contemplation of the open gate, and reached the passage again. The sense of unreality that had come the moment he had discovered that the others were gone was intensified. He had a feeling that it was a dream—a real dream—and that he would wake up. He even closed his eyes for a second and then opened them again, genuinely expecting to find his orderly bedroom and the sun shining through the window.

He was disappointed, for there was just the gloom and the bare passage and a faint but definite smell of beer.

"Blast it!" said Dawlish.

"A pleasure," said the man's voice from behind him.

It came with a devastating suddenness, absolutely out of the blue, and Dawlish felt his heart turn over. The voice came from above him, somewhere up the stairs, and he tried to see the speaker. He failed. Silence reigned again, broken only by his heavy breathing. He did not try to pretend that he wasn't scared; he had never been so jumpy in his life.

But he had to speak again.

"That's nice of you," he said. "What are these? Parlor-tricks?"

"Croaker's tricks," said that voice. It was a deep, pleasant voice, the voice of any cultured man, and somehow it lacked the note of sinisterness that Dawlish had expected. The only thing he was sure about was that no woman could have spoken like that.

"The Croaker, eh?" His voice was dry. "Perhaps you'll introduce us?"

"In good time," said the man with the pleasant voice. "Put that gun away, will you?"

"I haven't got a gun."

"Lies won't help."

Dawlish shrugged his shoulders and held onto his gun. He took a half step forward, sheltered beneath the passage wall so that the man above him could not shoot. He was determined not to give in easily.

"Fool!" said the man. There was a sudden stab of flame, a sharp hiss, and a bullet plumped into the wall within an inch of Dawlish's right ear. And he had not dreamed there was anyone *in front of him*. That bullet had seemed to come from a blank wall.

Dawlish did the obvious and touched the trigger. A bullet spat out toward the spot where he had seen the flash of flame, but it struck against the wall and fell to the floor. The wall *was* blank.

"Getting worried?" asked the man who was speaking from the stairs—or somewhere above Dawlish. "It will be only a matter of seconds before you get something else if you don't drop that gun."

Dawlish hesitated for a fraction of a second, then he let the automatic go.

Dawlish felt very helpless as the gun clattered to the floor, and the thought of Cutter and the others flashed through his mind. He still had no idea at all what had happened to them. He thought of the possibility of a floor which had opened and swallowed them, but to go without a sound—no, that was impossible. He would have heard something.

The silence was unnerving. The man was no longer speaking, and the sound of the clattering automatic was still ringing in his ears. He looked toward the kitchen door, with longing in his heart. He would have given a great deal to have been able to get outside.

The light in the passage was switched on suddenly, and the glare was abrupt and painful. Dawlish's eyes were still closed when that pleasant voice came again.

"Now it's all right, my dear Dawlish."

Dawlish waited for a split second, and then opened his eyes. He was half prepared for the man standing in front of him. The man gave a deep, pleasant laugh.

"Well, Dawlish."

Two things flooded through Dawlish's mind, and both of them seemed all-important. First, that it was easy to understand why the police had not made many strides toward catching the Croaker, second that there was no chance of his getting away from here alive. Otherwise he would never have been allowed to set eyes on this man.

He had seen him several times, but remembered him best at the Towers just after the murder of Slip Deacon. He had heard Trivett talk of him a great deal, and he knew he was famous in his own way. A handsome, swarthy-faced man with a pair of gleaming gray eyes and a thin line of moustache. Named Charleton. *Superintendent Charleton,* who had pretended to tell Dawlish all that he had known about the Croaker.

Charleton, of the C.I.D., thin and well-knit, perfectly dressed and perfectly poised.

"You!" gasped Dawlish.

"How well you react to certain standards!" said Charleton. "I won't say I'm surprised, and you seem to be cut to type. What made you come here tonight?"

Dawlish recovered well, rubbed his broken nose, and smiled.

"Well—let's say an urge. I keep getting surprises, Superintendent."

"Don't you? It's surprising how many things surprise us, my dear Dawlish. I was surprised, for instance, to find you and your friends here, but I recovered from it."

"While on the subject of my friends, where are they?"

"Being well cared for. I wasn't anxious to see them, only you. Don't worry too much, Dawlish. I'm going to give you a sharp lesson—at the request of the Croaker—and after that I'm hoping you will keep away from our little scheme, shall we call it?"

"Cat-and-mouse, eh? How do you perform your executions, Charleton?"

"Usually with an air gun," said Charleton. "But I've told you you needn't worry, we're not going to execute you. We only put the dangerous ones away. Come upstairs."

Dawlish hesitated, and then turned in the wake of Superintendent Charleton of Scotland Yard. His mind was in a whirl, for this thing was getting more and more fantastic. The fact that Charleton *was* here was more easily understood than the disappearance of the four men, including Cutts—whose deep voice usually made itself heard—and the fact that he had been fired at from a blank wall.

He had seen no one but the "policeman" until that moment. Now he sensed someone was behind him. Glancing over his shoulder, he saw a small man with a gun in his hand. The man must have come from somewhere.

Charleton turned his head at the same time and laughed.

"Don't worry, Dawlish, we specialize in the unusual. That is why the Croaker is so remarkable. Men have been into this house, for instance, and gone out rather unpleasantly. It's queer how little is required to make some men mad."

Dawlish swallowed hard.

"I suppose so."

"No one takes much notice of a madman, Dawlish. Have you ever found that?"

"I've heard it rumored." Dawlish had to keep his voice level, but even then it was suspiciously harsh.

He could see what this man meant now, and it was almost too horrible to believe.

Visits to the pub could turn men mad.

He could believe that. But he could not believe his own sanity would ever be at stake. On the other hand, vile things could happen. He had been in Paraguay during the South American war, and he had been in the Congo. He knew what pain and torture could do, and he was feeling very cold.

They reached the top of the stairs and Dawlish found himself in a second narrow passage, but this time several doors opened out. Charleton passed two doors and stopped at the third. The little man poked his gun in Dawlish's ribs.

"Scram," said Dawlish, and he pushed the gun away.

He knew that it was asking for trouble, but it was also putting things to a test.

The man clipped Dawlish behind the ear. Dawlish swore, but the gun was very threatening, while Charleton had pushed open the door and was waiting for the prisoner to enter. Dawlish drew a deep breath and went in.

He stopped dead still.

Charleton laughed, and the little man with the gun pushed Dawlish farther into the room and closed the door, while three men stared at the newcomers, one of them with his face twisted in fear and the other two without expression, which proved that they felt hopeless.

Ted Beresford and Tony Rawling—and the man named Brenner, who had made this possible. They had failed to reach Sir Jeremy Pinkerton.

13

Mr. Dawlish Gets Answers

Dawlish's teeth were gleaming in what seemed to be an inane smile, and his hands were clenched by his side. Silence reigned for twenty seconds, before Beresford broke it.

"Hallo, Pat. You too?"

"He's made a good job of it," said Dawlish with a forced cheerfulness. "How are things, Tony? Gentlemen—meet Superintendent Charleton of Scotland Yard."

They stared unbelievingly at the policeman.

"I was just saying to Dawlish," he assured them cheerfully, "that the world is full of surprises but we usually get over them. However, the Croaker wants to see you, Dawlish. You have no objection, I hope."

Dawlish's tension eased.

"I'd be delighted," he said.

"In the next room. Before we go in I'd like you to see a little job we have to do. Schmidt!"

His voice hardened on the name, and he looked at the man who had pushed Dawlish's back a few seconds before. The man with the gun smiled—he was an indescribably ugly man, with a face like sin—and raised his gun. Brenner—forgotten until that moment—uttered a high-pitched scream and jumped forward.

There was just a hiss, a snap, and a stab of flame, and the

bullet took Brenner full in the chest. Only the one bullet was fired. Brenner did not make another sound, but his hands went upward and then he crashed to the floor.

"Brenner should have learned not to talk," said Charleton in that pleasant, conversational voice. "It's odd how some people take a lot of teaching, and others are easily taught. I——"

It was then that Dawlish acted, then that the whole thing changed, then that Beresford jumped forward with his eyes blazing and his fists clenched. For Dawlish could stand a certain amount, but to see anyone killed in cold blood was too much. He flung caution to the winds and leapt at Charleton. The man with the gun was taken by surprise and Charleton, taking a pile-driver on the chin, went flying backward into the murderer.

Charleton was off his balance, but he struggled to keep it, rooting for the gun in his pocket. But he had never known a man move like Dawlish moved then. The clenched right fist took him in the stomach, then something like a battering ram found his chin.

Bone cracked on bone, and Charleton left the floor and hit the wall before sliding down in an unconscious heap. The little gunman had managed to touch the trigger, but before the bullet stabbed out Beresford had hit him. Beresford had a punch that could knock out most men. There was an ominous crack as his head went back and his eyes rolled.

Beresford stopped, and Dawlish stared down at the unconscious Charleton. Neither of them felt as though he could believe what had happened. Rawling drew a deep breath and stepped forward, the first to break the strained silence.

"Nice work, sons," he said. "Charleton will feel sore in the morning, and we've two corpses. Ted, don't hit so hard when you hit me. Now what?"

Dawlish straightened up and laughed. It was not hysterical

but it was precious close to it. The strain had been greater than anything else he had ever faced.

"A cigarette," he said, "and I could do with a drink."

"What are you going to do with these?" Rawling asked.

Dawlish lit a cigarette and shook his head.

"I don't know. I don't know a thing," he added with emphasis. "Where's the Croaker? Where are the others? Why the blazes doesn't someone come?"

"Is that door locked?" asked Beresford unexpectedly.

It didn't seem real. There were the two dead men and the unconscious Charleton, the three of them sound in wind and limb and not a murmur from anyone else near by. And when Beresford tried the door the handle turned and the lock went back. It *wasn't* locked.

"Oh no," said Dawlish, "I don't believe it. Alice in Fairyland."

"He's got one," said Beresford, pointing to the man with the broken neck. He took the man's gun from his lifeless grasp, while Dawlish helped himself to an automatic from Charleton's pocket. Tony Rawling found a blackjack and swished it through the air.

"A blank wall fired at me five minutes ago," said Dawlish, "and Cutts and three heavyweights just disappeared. When we get outside the stairs won't be there, or the house will be missing."

He seemed to be walking on air as he went onto the landing and looked about him. That same unreal sensation, as though he knew it was a dream lingered. But the stairs were solid, and the two doors which he had passed with Charleton a few minutes before were open, too, and the rooms beyond were empty.

Dawlish went carefully, touching the floor ahead of him as he went. Nothing happened. He hesitated at the foot of the stairs and looked upward. There was a flight going up and another flight going down. Prudence suggested he go downward.

"You two stay here in case of accidents," he said. "Or, better, one of you get Charleton and drag him to the foot of the stairs. I'm going down."

"Let's all keep together," said Beresford, "we'll be safer."

"Bring Charleton," repeated Dawlish, and Beresford shrugged his shoulders. Like his friend, he was wondering whether this was real, and he seemed like someone taking a part in a fantasy. But by the time he had dragged the unconscious policeman from the room, Dawlish had returned from downstairs, looking dazed and uncertain.

"It's all safe and all solid," he said. "It gets worse. Or better. I wonder if we can find Cutts?"

And then the next thing happened, the incredible thing and something that made all three of them stop dead still at the head of the stairs and look at each other. For the voice came from the ceiling: they knew that. And there was something about it which seemed to curdle their blood. It was a deep, harsh voice, but the one thing that sprang to all their minds was the fact that it sounded like a croak.

The Croaker! . . .

"You can find Cutter. Downstairs in the cellar. Safe. Take Charleton with you."

The voice stopped as abruptly as it had started, and the silence that followed seemed like a shroud. Even Beresford, usually quick with his tongue, could find no words. It was Dawlish who spoke next, his voice a little high-pitched.

"Where did that voice come from?"

"It might have come from anywhere," said Rawling, pointing to the grille in the ceiling. They looked up, and saw that it might easily be a loudspeaker. The voice had certainly come from above them, and the only likely transmitter was that grille.

Dawlish's smile returned, almost full strength.

"So we go on," he said. "It would look as if there's a spot of bother between Charleton and the Croaker. Will you try to remember that voice, Ted?"

Beresford made a gesture that was not altogether polite, and the three of them went downstairs, leaving Charleton at the top. He would be all right for ten minutes and they were anxious to find out whether the man with the croaking voice had spoken the truth when he said that Cutts was in the cellar.

They reached the passage and saw the door that led to the cellar. The same door, Dawlish suddenly realized, through which the shot had been fired at him earlier on. It was built in the wall opposite which he had crouched, and while he had been holding his gun the little man who now had a broken neck had opened it, fired at him, and closed it again. No wonder it had seemed to come from a blank wall.

Beresford opened the door and pointed to the soft rubber at its edges. He pulled it to and it closed with hardly a sound.

"Two of us. We'll draw lots to see who stays up to keep guard," said Dawlish.

Rawling drew the unlucky end of a match broken in three. Dawlish led the way down the stairs, through a smell of beer and other things. At the bottom of the cellar they found electric switches, and as Dawlish clicked them on light flooded the large subterranean room.

Crates and barrels surrounded them, casks and racks of wine were ahead of and behind them. But Dawlish was not interested in beer at the moment. He wanted to find Cutter.

He went forward, stooping to avoid the beams that stretched across the cellar, toward a door let in the far wall.

He tried the handle, and it turned without any trouble. Like all the doors at the Magpie it opened silently. The light shed a dim glow into the second cellar before Dawlish pressed on a nearby switch, and the smaller compartment was flooded with a glare from an unshaded lamp.

And he found himself staring at Cutts, who was standing grimly in front of three heavyweights in mackintoshes, and holding an automatic in his right hand.

If Dawlish was surprised, Cutter was stupified. The light was shining immediately above him, showing the white of his pate beneath the few odd strands of hair, which had become disarranged.

Dawlish broke the tension.

"Ho, Cutts! Safe and sound, then?"

"How the perishing hell did you get here?" demanded Cutter in his vast bass voice. "You nearly had one through the middle."

"I'm used to ingratitude," said Dawlish cheerfully. "It's true, Ted, he's here. And"—his eyes were gleaming, and he licked his lips—"there's beer. Who's thirsty?"

It was typical of the young men who worked with Patrick Dawlish that they should quench their thirst first from a barrel of draught beer, which obligingly had a dozen clean glasses standing near.

"What happened to you?" Dawlish asked Cutts.

"It was damned funny, old boy. You were three yards ahead of us, and then a partition came down from the ceiling and cut the passage in two. Before I knew where I was, three or four gentlemen with guns had us in line and marched us down here."

Dawlish scratched his nose.

"And I'd told Ted there wasn't an explanation," he said. "Let's go and explore."

They went and explored. The dropping partition was made of padded rubber and absolutely soundproof. It was operated by pressing a button in the side of the stairs, and came down without a sound.

"They certainly like peace in the Magpie," Dawlish said. "But the thing is now—where's the Croaker?"

"A long way away," said Ted Beresford, his ugly face broken for once in a smile. "But we've learned something. The Croaker is well disposed toward us. Otherwise why the hell did he let us get away? We've queered his pitch at the Greet Club, we've pestered him generally, yet he gets us in a spot as he did tonight and then lets us go. I wonder why?"

14

Round Table

They all wondered why, but none could offer any suggestions. It was a plain fact that they were lucky to have escaped with their lives, and it was equally plain that for some reason the Croaker had allowed them to escape.

Dawlish phoned the Yard—without finding Trivett in—and told a startled inspector that there were two dead men and an unconscious one at the Magpie. The unconscious one was name Charleton, and whatever happened he was not to be allowed to go free. Five minutes later he found himself talking to a bad-tempered assistant-commissioner, who had been hauled out of bed.

The A.C. was a friend of a friend of Pat Dawlish's, and easily smoothed. At first he flatly refused to believe the Charleton story.

"Three of us can give evidence," Dawlish said, "so don't let the man get away. You might be able to learn something worthwhile, too, for Charleton will have no love for the Croaker now."

By the time Dawlish and the others were at the Clarge Street flat the police were at the Magpie in full strength, and the truth of part of Dawlish's story was proved.

Dawlish dropped into an easy chair as soon as he reached the flat. The room looked a mess, for no one had cleared up after the Brenner episode, but no one minded that.

Dawlish eyed Beresford thoughtfully.

"Which reminds me, you've something to explain. What happened after you left here?"

Beresford grimaced, and his face looked more homely than ever.

"Caught for a mug," he said. "A man stepped off the pavement almost in front of me. I pulled up and let rip, and the swab stood up and showed a gun. A brace of others came quickly. Tony and I hadn't a chance, and with a gun in my ribs I drove to the Magpie. That reminds me, there ought to be a car near somewhere. I forgot the damned thing."

Dawlish grinned.

"The Croaker probably took a liking to it. It practically proves that no one—not even the girl—was taken in when I said that I was Number Seventeen, and it proves the Croaker doesn't kill for the sake of it. He doesn't kill just for vengeance. I wish I knew who that girl was."

"So do I," said Beresford, who looked worried. "And the man Morelli—didn't I hear you mention the name?"

"You did. Brenner used it, but if the girl is Morelli I'll eat my hat. It's a name we can watch for. And we've got to start again."

"You're going on?" asked Cutts.

"Of course. Why not?"

"I wondered," said Cutter slowly, and chuckled. "We aren't likely to get away with that again, Pat."

"No-o. But we're getting experience. The Croaker won't expect us to cry enough."

"No idea yet who the Croaker is?" asked Cutter.

"None at all. Have you?" There was something behind Cutter's comments which Dawlish couldn't fathom. But Cutter shook his head and said, suddenly, that he was tired.

"We'll sleep here," said Dawlish, "unless anyone particularly wants to go home, and we can have a round table at breakfast. There's one thing," he added, "we've no responsibilities at the moment, and Uncle Jeremy will miss his sleeping partners."

"Ah," said Wishart Cutter, but he said it under his breath and looked at Tony Rawling. Tony closed one eye, very slowly, and yawned to hide the effect.

They were thinking strange things about Sir Jeremy Pinkerton, but preferred not to say a word.

The "burglars" whom Cutter had hired on the previous night were paid their fifty pounds apiece, and asked for more action, so that they could earn it.

Particularly one Eric, a man as large as Dawlish, also with a broken nose. There was no "little" about Eric. He looked the beefiest customer who had ever stepped into the ring and also he looked villainous. Cutter recommended him as the gentlest man in the East End, although he could do remarkable things to a bar of iron.

At ten o'clock the next morning Eric arrived, looking more than a little sheepish. He had not, he claimed, earned his fifty quid. He had a slight impediment in his speech that contrasted strangely with his appearance.

"C'n I stay here?" he lisped. "Kinda keep a watch, Mr. Dawlish? Pritty useful and I c'n serve at the table. 'Ad three yers with a family befaw the war."

Dawlish finished toweling and selected a shirt.

"Offering me your services, Eric?"

"Shure. Useful, too." Eric doubled an arm, and the cloth of his coat threatened to split. "Oke?"

"Oke," said Pat Dawlish, and they shook hands on it. Dawlish wanted a man anyhow, and if Eric was not the apple of a valet's eye he certainly would prove useful. Moreover, he would be a contact between the flat and the club near the Magpie.

Astonishing things happened in the next half hour. A pile of dirty crockery disappeared and became clean. Clothes were brushed and trousers were pressed. Things which were where they should not be were righted. Four young men followed Eric about the flat, wide-eyed, and asked how it was done, while the mountainous ex-boxer moved with incredible silence in his hobnailed boots, and hummed beneath his breath. When the knock came at the door—and the others were at last fully clad, and prepared for business—he reached it before any of them, and they heard his respectful lisping:

"Good morning, sir."

"Mr. Dawlish?" said Chief-Inspector Trivett of Scotland Yard.

"If you will please come this way, sir," said Eric, and he ushered Trivett into the room.

Trivett eyed the quartet without speaking for a moment, and accepted a cigarette. Beresford jumped from a chair and bowed before the inspector, and Trivett had an idea that these men should really have been born fools. Only Beresford, with a slightly wounded left shoulder, had suffered in the brawl at the Greet Club or the affair at the Magpie, and the others showed no traces at all of a late night or its consequences. Dawlish looked innocent and still a little inane, and Trivett, after a moment's awkward silence, suddenly laughed.

Eric displayed pleasing acumen in bringing beer.

"Where did you get him from?" Trivett asked as the giant padded out.

"A gift," said Dawlish, and he explained. He went on to recount the affair of the night before, and Trivett showed his wisdom by accepting it all as gospel. The only time he frowned was when Charleton was mentioned.

"Of course, that was just bloody," he said. "No one sus-pected——"

"Has he been working for the Croaker for long?"

"Eighteen months, he says. He's told everything he knows, but that's little more than we do. That the Croaker croaks. That there's a woman in it somewhere. That his headquarters were for some time at the Magpie——"

"They're not now, of course," said Beresford.

"Don't listen to him," implored Dawlish. "He's congenital. You've been to the Magpie this morning?"

"We have," said Trivett, scratching his chin. "The daily staff arrived about eight o'clock, but none of them know a thing—they say—about the Croaker. None of them ever sleep there, not even the manager. The owner did. A man named——"

"Morelli?" suggested Pat Dawlish gently.

"How the blazes did you know?"

"Brenner whispered it to me. The man who was shot last night. And of course Morelli has now disappeared. Tell me, Bill, have you ever heard of a man called the Speaker?"

"Only one," said Trivett. "He works at Westminster."

"Then you haven't heard of this fellow. Brenner said that Morelli was the Speaker, but I also heard the girl. Well, there isn't much to say, unless you'll want us to give inquest evidence of a sort about the two dead men."

"And Charleton," said Trivett, frowning. "And I'll have to worry you for a complete signed statement of what happened last night. Don't forget anything, for heaven's sake, because this thing is now getting serious."

"Getting!" scoffed Pat Dawlish, but he obliged with the statement, using a portable typewriter for legibility. It was signed by the others, and Trivett took his leave, worried and puzzled.

"Now what?" asked Cutter sepulchrally.

"Several pointers," said Dawlish. "First, Lady Pelisse and her Percy. Second, Joan Fayre. Shut up, Ted. Third, Fayre *père* and the other three members of the syndicate. We ought to be able to trace them. Then there are the unknowns or the missing ones. Morelli—Eric might be able to help us get a line on him. Greet. And of course the Speaker and the Croaker, and the girl who spoke to me on the telephone last night. Hers was a voice I'd never forget again, and that's not imagination. Ted, I'm sorry, but I want to handle the angle of Joan Fayre, and I'll take Cutts with me. Leave La Grana alone, but snoop round Sir Charles Faversham, will you?"

Beresford said that he would and left the flat, ushered out with Tony Rawling for company and Eric as a footman. Dawlish and Cutter—who went hatless despite his sparse hair —went out soon afterward, an interview with Joan Fayre as their object in view. Dawlish saw a way in which the various angles of the affair could be checked up now, and he did not propose to leave anything undone.

Dawlish was hoping that he would not recognize Joan Fayre's voice as that of the woman on the telephone on the previous night, for he knew that Ted had fallen for the girl. He had no opportunity of proving it one way or the other. For when he reached the house he found a pale, speechless Horatio Fayre gnawing at his thick white moustache, and staring about him with haggard eyes.

Dawlish learned that Joan Fayre was missing.

15

The Missing Heiress

Horatio Fayre's voice was on a monotonous level as he told Dawlish what had happened. It was probable, Dawlish knew, that Fayre would have told the story to anyone who showed the slightest interest, for the millionaire was suffering from a severe shock.

"She didn't come back from the Greet Club," Fayre muttered. "We left there together after Greet, but I lost her downstairs and since then I haven't seen her. It's more than I can stand, Dawlish."

He broke off suddenly and Dawlish saw the expression of uncertainty, almost of fear, that passed through his eyes. Dawlish saw that his eyes were a light brown, almost amber. Weak eyes and more those of an animal than a man—a queer fact, for there was nothing at all bestial about the mild-mannered millionaire.

But he was afraid that he had said too much.

Dawlish could almost see him putting the brakes on, and he came to the conclusion that there were things on Mr. Fayre's mind that were not for publication. But for the fact that Trivett had been sure the man was interested in the Greet Club, Dawlish might have suspected nothing. As it was, he wondered just why Fayre was afraid that he would open his mouth too much.

Something of the desperation went out of Fayre's voice.

"Of course it's a shock, but probably she's run off with someone—girls do, although I would never have thought it of Joan. You'll appreciate the need for keeping it absolutely to yourself, Mr. Dawlish?"

"Yes," said Dawlish. They were in the drawing room of the millionaire's Regent's Park house. "You seriously think she may have eloped?"

"We-ell—these things do happen." Fayre was biting his lip, and his hands were trembling, but he managed to keep his voice steady. "Of course it may be loss of memory—even a night escapade—nothing that requires publicity."

"You'll tell the police, of course?" said Dawlish.

He saw the way the man's lips tightened, saw those queer amber eyes narrow, and was more than ever convinced that Horatio Fayre was afraid—and afraid of the police among other things.

"The—police? Don't be a fool, man, they——"

"Supposing it is loss of memory, supposing even that it's a case of kidnapping?" suggested Dawlish, leaning back in an easy chair and taking out his cigarette case. "If you don't advise the police immediately there's a chance that serious damage will be done. You want to find your daughter, don't you?"

"And I'll find her in my own way," snapped Fayre. It was easier to see now how this man could control the many boards of which he was chairman, and possible to imagine why he was a financial wizard with a reputation for quick decisions and unusual stubbornness. "I hope I do not need to stress that, sir."

Dawlish withdrew a rejected cigarette case and selected a cigarette with a care that was deliberate and annoying.

"I hope so too," he said. "You know the Croaker raided the Greet Club last night?"

"Yes." Short, sharp, and decisive, and no apparent reaction to the mention of the Croaker.

"You know the Croaker well?"

"Only what I have heard of him in the press," said Fayre. "Why?"

"He's capable of murder," said Dawlish. "And worse. I had an idea that you might think the Croaker could tell you where to find Joan."

"And what made you think of it?" There was no change in that set, almost basilisk expression, and Dawlish realized that Fayre needed sharp watching. He had been frightened by the disappearance of his daughter, and he was afraid for her. But for some reason which it was not easy to understand he was more afraid of something else, and the last thing he wanted was publicity.

"Just the fact that she disappeared with the Croaker's men," smiled Dawlish. "But, of course, so did you."

"Nonsense! I was near the door and so was Joan. We——"

"A father's first thought," protested Dawlish gently, "is the safety of his daughter. You were very anxious indeed to get away, weren't you? No thought of women and children first, for instance?"

There was a calculated insult in the words, for Dawlish wanted to get under Fayre's skin, and from the way in which the little man's pale cheeks colored, it seemed as though he was near success.

"You're impertinent, Dawlish. What brought you?"

"Curiosity," smiled Dawlish genially. "I'm looking for the Croaker—but perhaps you knew that—and I had an idea Joan knew him."

The restraint which the millionaire was exercising broke with a sudden fury. Fayre jumped to his feet and stood over Dawlish, his fists raised, his legs set apart.

"You damnably impertinent upstart, get out of here! Joan and the Croaker—you fool, you fool! She knows nothing about him, she's never even heard of him. I've made sure——"

Fayre broke off suddenly, and turned color. Dawlish stared up at the man very grimly.

"What have you made sure of, Fayre?"

"No-nothing. I've made sure Joan has never mixed with unpleasant company; it's impossible that she should have come in contact with the Croaker. Dawlish, I'm so worried that I hardly know what I'm saying. If I've offended you, please consider it withdrawn. If I could only find Joan."

Dawlish shrugged his shoulders, and his voice was relaxed.

"How long has she been missing?"

"Well—since eleven o'clock last night or a little later. After the Greet Club raid."

"She's never been missing for the same period before?"

"Not without advising me—no."

"Were you on good terms with her?"

"Yes, yes, of course. I had to make sure that her youthful spirits did not lead to indiscretions, of course. I was annoyed last night to find her at the club, and I said so. But apart from an occasional and necessary parental correction we have been excellent friends."

"And you want to see her alive again?"

Fayre did not answer immediately; when he did speak his voice was hoarse.

"My dear Dawlish, that's an absurd question. Of course I do. I don't think she is in danger of her life——"

"I don't think you deserve to see her again," said Dawlish heavily. "You're lying and you keep on lying. If you want to make sure she's all right, go to the police. They can help you. No one else can."

Fayre stood like a statue, staring down at Dawlish—and believing him. Dawlish was quite sure of that. The man *believed* that he would not see his daughter again. Yet she had only been missing for a few hours.

Then Fayre turned abruptly on his heel.

"That's enough. You are impertinent, Dawlish!"

Dawlish stood up suddenly to his full height. "I'm going straight from here to the Yard. I'm going to tell them all I know, and every police station in England will be warned to keep a lookout for your daughter. You may like to take a chance on her return, but I prefer not to. And I'm going to give the story to the press. Understand?"

Horatio Fayre understood; and Dawlish was appalled, for he slipped his hand into his coat pocket. Dawlish saw it going but didn't expect what came out. Fayre had a gun, and its ugly snout was pointing at Dawlish.

Dawlish stared at the gun and the man holding it, simply unable to believe that it was really happening. Fayre with a gun. A millionaire taking the chance of holding a visitor up on his own premises. It was madness. . . .

"You understand, Dawlish, that I can't allow any such thing. This matter is private, and I have not the slightest desire for publicity."

"You'll get some if you shoot," Dawlish said.

"That's a matter of opinion. I don't want to shoot, but I will if necessary. Understand? No word of Joan's disappearance must reach the police or the press."

"Keep insisting," said Dawlish, and he yawned. As he yawned he put his hand to his mouth and then, without giving a second's warning, he jumped forward.

At the same moment Fayre touched the trigger of his gun.

Dawlish actually saw the man's trigger finger move, and he heard the sudden hiss just as he expected from a silenced automatic. But there was no flame, although something tore through his right arm as he went forward.

He was going through the air like a battering ram, and Fayre lost his nerve, turned, and tried to run. Dawlish crashed into him and they went down together. Dawlish banged his knee and the pain was excruciating. If Fayre had found his courage again, the big man could have done nothing. Every bit of wind was knocked out of the millionaire's body, and he was lying still as Dawlish scrambled to his feet.

Dawlish was pale. It had been a closer thing than he liked, and somehow the fact that *Fayre* had fired made him more worried. He would have expected it of a lot of people, but that mild little man—no, it didn't seem credible. He heard a gasp, and looked up quickly. He caught a glimpse of a man hurrying away from the window of the drawing room. He saw that Fayre was stretched out in a queer position, different from what he had been five seconds before.

Dawlish felt as if a squall had hit him. He felt winded and buffeted and off his balance, but the association of ideas came quickly and he knew his first job was to try and get the man who was now hurrying along the short drive of the house. He reached the window and pushed it up, but before he could jump out the man had reached the gates, and the engine of a car started up.

Dawlish knew it was useless to follow. The car would reach a bend in the road before he could get to the gates and he would not be able to see even what make or model it was. He felt sick as he turned back to the drawing room, climbed in, and turned Horatio Fayre over.

At the side of Fayre's forehead was a small round hole, drilled by a bullet from an air gun. The same method of killing, the same type of weapon that had been used on Slip Deacon.

And then Dawlish went stiff and looked at the gun in his hand. It had shown no flame when it had been fired, and now he knew why. Fayre had owned one of those powerful air guns. *Fayre* had been prepared to kill as the Croaker had killed!

16

Murder of M.P.'s

Dawlish realized that Fayre had been shot with a bullet from a gun identical with that which he was holding in his hand, making a case for the police if they cared to be funny, and for a moment he played with the idea of getting out while he could.

There was nothing he could do for Fayre, who had died instantaneously. But there might be something he could do for his daughter, and there might be papers in Fayre's rooms giving some idea of what he had known.

Dawlish strode to the door and pulled it open.

As he reached the hall the footman eyed him so nervously that Dawlish wondered what the man had seen or heard.

"Who's the family doctor?"

"Dr.—Dr. Mendor, sir. Is—is there anything——"

"The matter, yes," said Dawlish, wishing that he could have called a police surgeon. "How many telephones in the house?"

"Three extensions, sir, but only one line."

"I want the telephone. You go and get Dr. Mendor, will you? Or send one of the servants. Where's Mr. Fayre's study?"

"On the first floor, sir. But——"

"Hurry for the doctor," said Dawlish quickly. "I'm going to telephone the police. Don't say a word to another soul, and lock the drawing-room door."

He spoke as though he did not doubt for a moment that he

would be obeyed, and the mention of the police gave confidence. The footman slipped a key from the inside of the drawing-room door, glancing quickly at the outstretched body of his employer, locked the door, and pocketed the key before turning away. Dawlish started up the stairs.

There were a dozen things he wanted to know, but he controlled his thoughts for the moment. First the study, then the police. With any luck, and assuming there was no one upstairs to interfere, he could run through the papers in the desk and cupboards of the study. There would be a safe, of course, but it needed Eric's friend to open it.

Without appearing to hurry he searched the drawers of a heavy antique desk, a filing cabinet, and two small cupboards, to find a host of papers and a lot of interesting information, but nothing concerning the Croaker. There was a small safe let in the wall, and he regarded it lingeringly.

Then he looked at the telephone.

It was on the desk, near the chair in which Fayre must have been sitting not long before. And—Dawlish's eyes glistened—so was a case of keys.

He singled out the smallest and tried it on the safe. It worked. He told himself as he swung the door open that Fayre had been in a terribly worried frame of mind to leave the keys about, and also that he had probably taken a telephone message only a short while before he had left the study.

Dawlish took the little bundle of papers from inside the safe. It was surprising that there was nothing else there. No valuables, no money that he could see. Just a dozen or so papers rolled and fastened with a rubber band. He slipped the band off quickly and sorted the papers out, and then he stared down, his face set and his eyes gleaming.

For they were letters and statements of accounts between the five members of the syndicate which had run the Greet

Club. And the profits in the course of eighteen months had run close on half a million pounds.

"Of course," said Chief-Inspector William Trivett, "you're a damned fool. You've not only admitted holding a gun with one bullet—or slug if you like—missing, but you've admitted running through Fayre's papers."

"I'll take what comes," said Dawlish. "And I've a hole in my right sleeve which will show you where one slug went. Apart from that—what do you think of the papers and the Greet Club?"

Trivett pushed his hand through his dark hair.

Dawlish believed the man was feeling more worried than he looked. The ground had been jolted from under his feet by the treachery of Superintendent Charleton. He was groping in the dark now, and the murder of Horatio Fayre made the groping more blind.

"We had information—anonymously—about the five members of the syndicate. And we were also told that it was connected with the Croaker. Nothing definite, of course—that's why I passed the names over to you; they weren't official. Now we've all the proof we want that two Members of Parliament and two millionaires, with a peer of the realm, ran the gambling racket, and it won't make a pleasant taste in the mouths of the People Who Matter."

"Why did the Croaker kill Fayre?" asked Dawlish.

Trivett looked somber.

"Obviously for the same reason that he killed Pelisse, and I don't like it a bit. The whole affair is getting grim. If he'd killed you I could have understood it more. He's killing anyone who's dangerous. But to let you go——"

"I'm sorry I disappointed you," said Dawlish, dryly. "The Croaker let me off for a reason quite unknown and I assure you I haven't any influence with the gentleman."

Trivett looked taken aback.

"I didn't think you had, but——"

"Does anyone else think so?"

Trivett lowered his voice to a confidential whisper. They were in the study at the dead millionaire's house, and the papers which Dawlish had found were on the desk between them. Dawlish had persuaded a servant to bring whisky, and he was smoking. Belowstairs the men from the Yard were carrying out the necessary formalities, and Sergeant Munk was in charge. The family doctor had not yet arrived, but the local police surgeon had been and gone, pronouncing the obvious cause of death.

"I don't think you're mixed up with the Croaker," said Trivett. "But, I've been told to watch you carefully. And your friends. And when this gets to the Commissioner's ears I wouldn't like to hear what he'll say."

Dawlish was still smiling.

"I see. And it looks as though this killing could be blamed on me?"

"No one can *prove* you didn't kill Fayre," said Trivett uncomfortably.

"One man can—the gentleman who shot him," said Dawlish. "And there's only one slug missing from that air gun, while two were fired. One through my arm, the other through Fayre's head."

"Let's see your arm," asked Trivett.

Dawlish obliged, and the policeman's face cleared. The wound was not a severe one, for the slug had gone clean through the fleshy part of the forearm. It had bled a little.

"Good, that's good. They'll have found the second slug downstairs now. Well, we still don't know really why Fayre was killed."

"Isn't it obvious?" asked Patrick Dawlish gently, and Trivett stared.

"Obvious? Why?"

"Because he was a member of the Greet Club syndicate," said Dawlish.

"Good—God!" Trivett swung around to the telephone as Dawlish went to the window.

He heard Trivett ask for the Yard and talking to the Assistant Commissioner. He heard the warning that the two Members of Parliament might be on the spot next, and gathered from Trivett's answers to the man at the other end of the wire that the suggestion was being taken seriously.

He could see the drive and the road in which Fayre's house was built as he stared out the window, and he saw the small car which turned in and pulled up opposite the front door. He was still smiling, a little oddly, for it was queer to feel that anyone suspected him of being associated with the Croaker. And then he tightened his lips, for he saw the tall, lean, Southern-looking man who climbed from the car, and recognized him. It was Dr. Mendor, who had been the divisional surgeon at Guildford months before—the man who had been called to the Towers when Slip Deacon had been murdered.

It was odd—so odd that Dawlish's mind started to do queer things. So did Trivett's when the news was passed on. Trivett had hardly replaced the receiver before Dawlish told him, and the Inspector whistled between set teeth.

"*Mendor,* eh? I knew he had left Guildford, but this is a new angle. Fayre would have a fashionable doctor."

"Or he might have used Mendor for other reasons," said Dawlish.

"You say you saw the back of the man who killed Fayre," asked Trivett.

"I did."

"Tall and thin, didn't you say?"

"You mean Mendor?"

"Get a back view of him and make sure if you can," said Trivett. "Don't come downstairs yet, but wait until he leaves. You can be watching from the head of the stairs."

"I'd get a wrong perspective," said Dawlish. "I'll wait by one of the doors down there."

He waited for fifteen minutes, and began to wonder whether his patience would last out when the door of the room where Fayre had been murdered opened. Trivett came out, with Mendor, lean and dark and smiling as ever. Dawlish recognized that rather sing-song voice immediately.

"A very sad business, Trivett, very sad indeed. Strange that I should meet with a Croaker crime again. Are you getting far with that affair?"

"It's progressing," said Trivett heavily.

They walked to the door, and Dawlish was prepared to swear that the man who had run from the window had been Mendor.

Mendor had shot Horatio Fayre.

It was on the tip of his tongue to call out then, but he stopped himself. Mendor left, and Trivett turned back, his face glum. Dawlish went forward thoughtfully.

"I think——" he started, but Trivett shook his head.

"Mendor's got a perfect alibi, so your imagination's letting you down. He was in Guildford, at the police station, two hours ago. Fayre's been dead an hour, and no car made could have done the journey in time to bring Mendor here when Fayre was killed."

He hurried upstairs as the phone burred out, and Dawlish followed. Neither of them knew what to expect—in fact, Dawlish had anticipated that it would be for someone in the house. But he was wrong, for the call was for Trivett, and it brought bad news. Dawlish saw the policeman's lips tighten, and heard him say:

"*Both* of them."

"Both of them," said the policeman at the other end of the wire. "And the murder of two M.P.'s is going to cause the biggest row yet."

17

Said Eric

Dawlish had seen the likelihood that the whole syndicate that had run the gaming club in Clarge Street would be victims of the Croaker, but he had taken it calmly, almost as if he did not seriously consider it likely that two Members of Parliament would be killed.

Only Faversham, that military- and distinguished-looking gentleman, was spared now. And would his turn come soon?

That possibility flashed through Dawlish's mind as Trivett banged down the telephone and looked around. There were shadows under the policeman's eyes.

"You heard?"

"I did. You've told them to look after Faversham?"

Trivett's laugh was like a bark.

"I've told them to look after the others. After Pelisse was murdered the other four have been followed everywhere by our men, but—they had no trouble in dodging them. They weren't trailed to the Greet Club the other night, for instance. They lost their trailers before that."

"And you've a man supposed to be watching Faversham now, have you?" asked Dawlish.

"I have. Faversham went into Essex this afternoon—he has a small house there. Two of our sergeants went after him, but God knows whether he's safe."

"Where were the others killed?" Dawlish asked gently, and he could see from the expression in the policeman's eyes that it was a sore point. But Trivett answered quickly if glumly.

"At their flat—they shared a flat, you know."

"I didn't know," admitted Dawlish. "But if they were followed, their flat was surely being watched?"

"They were believed to be at the House," said Trivett bitterly. "They must have slipped out before our men learned about it. It's lucky for you the other pellet's turned up, or you would be in Queer Street."

"The luck of the Dawlishes," murmured Patrick Dawlish; but he was still worried by the fact that he was not above suspicion. If Trivett had had orders to keep a watchful eye on him and the other three, that suggested that they were being followed wherever they went. In fact, a man should have followed Dawlish to Fayre's house.

He asked whether that had been done, and Trivett shrugged his shoulders.

"It should have been. But it's not always easy to keep a man in sight, and—well, let's face facts. After Charleton I don't see how we can rely on anyone. If there's one leak at the Yard there might well be a dozen."

Dawlish nodded slowly.

"Munk found the other slug downstairs, did he?"

"Yes. Well, I'm going to the Yard. If you're wise you'll retire to the country for a few weeks."

Dawlish chuckled.

"Until it's all over?"

"That's the idea."

"It's turned down with enthusiasm," said Dawlish; and Trivett, seeing those white teeth flashing and that blond hair shining in the December sun which found its way into the study, could not be sure whether the man was a fool who had had some luck or a clever man who was acting a part.

110

Dawlish was thoughtful as he left the house. Before they stepped from the porch of Fayre's home three reporters came up, and the servants were likely to have a warm time.

Dawlish walked from Bond Street to his flat, to find Eric, huge and soft-footed, ready with a cold lunch. From some mysterious place the ex-fighter had found shoes that fitted him and clothes that became a gentleman's gentleman. He was smiling as Dawlish entered.

"Well, Eric? Anything happened?"

"The telephone, sir," lisped Eric, "has been ringing." He continued to lisp, but his Cockney accent was gone—a surprising fact.

"Take any names?"

"No, sir. A lady telephoned and said she would be ringing again. Mr. Beresford telephoned, sir, to say that he has gone to Essex, after Sir Charles Faversham."

Dawlish's eyes kindled.

"Good for Ted. Any word from Mr. Cutter?"

"No, sir."

"Thanks." Dawlish lit a cigarette, and found beer at his elbow. Eric was more than a find, he was a genius. Dawlish drank, surveyed edibles, and pondered for a few minutes before setting to—there were so many things to ponder that he could not manage them all while eating alone.

Cutter had set out with him to visit Fayre, but Dawlish had decided, after all, to let the ex-lightweight go to the gymnasium in Aldgate High Street. Things had happened on the previous night which had not been reported, and it was as well they should be cleared up soon.

Queer things, when Dawlish brooded over them.

It seemed an age since the previous night and the affair at the Magpie, but some things stood out clearly. The affair of the sliding partition and the softly opening door, the microphone or loudspeaker, and the regular servants at the Magpie, all those things could and would be handled by the police. Trivett should know soon whether the voice which had come from the grille in the ceiling had been uttered in the pub. More likely in the pub, Dawlish thought.

It had been strange that the Magpie had emptied so completely. The girl who had spoken to him over the telephone, the Croaker, and perhaps Morelli—all of them had disappeared. But it was not unreasonable to assume that they had been at the Magpie some time on the previous evening.

How had they got out?

Two men had left the pub, and had been followed by two of Cutter's friends—Cutter should be back soon to report what they had done and where they had been. Then two men had been on guard outside the Magpie while the shindig had been going on, but they had heard and seen nothing. Cutter would confirm that this morning, anyhow.

When Ted Beresford and Tony Rawling had been held up, Brenner had had a companion, a wounded man. The man was missing and Dawlish wondered whether he was likely to be found again.

"Now—two things of importance," mused Dawlish. "Why did the Croaker send two men to the flat to bump me off and then let me go? And why did Lady Pelisse have a threatening note from the Croaker?"

"If I may suggest, sir," said a voice from Dawlish's elbow, "the threat might have been to *Sir Hugo,* sir."

"What the hell!" jerked Dawlish, and then he scowled as he saw Eric towering above him and holding a bottle. Eric's by no means handsome face was set in repose, and the man was bowing a little from the waist. "I'd forgotten you. So you think the note in La Grana's bag might have been Hugo?"

"It seems possible, sir," said Eric, controlling his Cockney accent admirably. Dawlish had come to the conclusion that earlier on Eric had assumed the Cockney, and was now talking naturally. There were a number of important questions in his mind about Eric.

"Yes," admitted Dawlish. "In fact, she might have opened the letter and kept it herself."

"Possibly, sir," said Eric. "I have known stranger things. I happen to know, sir, that Lord and Lady Pelisse were by no means a happily married couple."

"The devil you do!" exclaimed Dawlish, but his eyes were gleaming. "Where did you learn this?"

"One of the maids at Lanster Place. Lord and Lady Pelisse frequently quarreled, sir."

Dawlish swallowed more beer, not altogether because he was thirsty, but because Eric's remarks might prove useful.

"Over what?"

"Lady Pelisse, sir, is hardly what one might call morally irreproachable," announced Eric grandiosely. "Not exactly a *loose* woman, sir, but you will probably get what I mean."

Dawlish said that he did, and:

"Who taught you elocution, Eric?"

"My mother, sir," said the giant, who had once been more than a hope of British heavyweight boxing, and Dawlish had to stifle a laugh. "I learned a great deal about Lord and Lady Pelisse."

Dawlish's eyes were hard.

"*Did* you, Eric. You can't by any chance tell me any of the places where Lady Pelisse is apt to go—was, should I say—when she wanted to avoid her husband? Wanted, Eric—overlook the present tense."

"Yes, I can give you that information. Understanding, sir, that Lady Naida was in some way connected with the—er—murders, sir, I ventured to telephone the Lanster Place house this morning, and talked to Maude. The maid I know, sir, and

113

we hope one day to be spli—married, sir. There are two addresses, sir, and telephone numbers. Regent 81821 and Westminster 91293. Both are hotels."

"You don't happen to know the name of the Croaker, do you?" Dawlish asked.

Eric, mountainous, dignified and with that queer soft voice of his, with its broad vowels and soft consonants, shook his head.

"I think it quite safe to say that no one knows that."

"Not even his friends?"

"Not even his friends," agreed Eric. "I have heard the sobriquet mentioned a thousand times, and heard a hundred conversations about him, but no one has claimed to know him."

"Unpopular because he poaches, eh?"

"And because of what happens when anyone is foolish enough to defy him, sir. Quite a lot of people have been killed by the Croaker."

"And more to come, eh?" Dawlish's jaw seemed to stick out a mile. "Eric, we've got to move fast. I wish Cutts would come. I suppose you can't think of any reason why we were allowed to escape from the Magpie?"

Eric's face showed something like expression for the first time. He leaned forward and lowered his voice, and his incredibly battered nose seemed to move a little as he spoke.

"I can make a suggestion, sir. The moment you were allowed to go free you were under suspicion. The Croaker would like to see you—and your friends—in the hands of the police, sir. He works with a gang. And you and your three friends make quite a gang, sir, one that is interested in the Croaker. I thought of that the moment I heard you had escaped, because the Croaker works like that. And the police are suspicious because while you were out this morning three men came—genuine policemen to search your flat. I refused to let them, sir."

114

Dawlish's eyes were gleaming.

"So they tried and you stopped 'em, Eric." He was speaking very softly, and rubbing his forefinger round his chin. "How did you manage it with genuine policemen?"

Eric's expression changed again: this time he smiled, with almost seraphic contentment.

"In view of the times the Croaker's men have impersonated the police, sir, I took the liberty of assuming they were masqueraders. They were extremely surprised, I may say. They're in the bathroom. Would you care to see them?"

18

The Telephone Voice

Dawlish stared at the ex-boxer-manservant, his mouth a little agape and his blond hair ruffled, and in his blue eyes an expression of blank amazement.

"Good God!" he gasped. "Eric, that won't do. Three dicks in my bathroom——"

"Bound and gagged."

Dawlish stood up slowly, like a man trying to imitate slow motion.

"You know, this gets worse," he said. "I don't know whether I dare trust you alone. Let them out."

"Certainly, sir."

Dawlish still felt as if the ground had been taken from under his feet. It was one thing to argue with a policeman, but to lock three in a bathroom for hours on end was asking for trouble.

But there was a humor in it and he was starting to laugh when two things happened at the same time. The front doorbell rang and the telephone burred out.

Obviously Eric had no regard for the three men in the bathroom. He reached the bathroom door, but swung around on his heel and marched out of the room to the front door, while Dawlish took up the telephone. This might be from Trivett or a dozen people, it——

"Mr. Dawlish?"

Dawlish hardly knew why it came with such a shock, but it was the biggest he had had since he had first started to try and find the Croaker. For this was a girl's voice, a light, lilting, lovely voice—the voice of the woman who had telephoned from the Magpie on the previous night.

Dawlish drew a deep breath, and the girl said: "Hallo."

"Hallo," said Dawlish heavily. "Mrs. Speaker?"

The girl at the other end of the wire laughed.

"I wondered if you'd recognize me. I'm telephoning on instructions, Mr. Dawlish."

"Call me 'Pat'," urged Dawlish. "Do you prefer 'Joan'?"

"Joan? Why Joan?"

"Thoughts," said Dawlish, and he pulled himself together. "Well, what can I do for you?"

"Telephone your friend Beresford at the Red Calf in Chelmsford," said the girl with the voice like an angel's, "and tell him to keep away from Sir Charles Faversham. Faversham is not a safe bet at the moment."

"Beresford and Rawling," Dawlish said heavily, "are usually able to take care of themselves."

"But they're not used to working against the Croaker," said the girl at the other end of the wire. "He has been very good to you, but I doubt whether his patience will last much longer."

"I'm not as grateful as I might be." Dawlish's voice was hard. "I wish to God I could get my hands on you."

"You won't," said the girl sweetly. "You will never have the pleasure of meeting me, Mr. Dawlish. I've seen you several times, of course——"

"Of course?"

"You patronize the Carlton when you're in London, don't you? I've seen you there. And I've rather taken a liking to you. Otherwise you would not have been so fortunate last night."

"So it's you I have to thank, not the Croaker," said Dawlish dryly.

"Maybe, if you're wise you'll recall Beresford and Rawling."

"I was thinking of going down to join them," said Dawlish.

"You mustn't do that—whatever happens you mustn't do that!"

"I see," said Pat Dawlish heavily. "All right, I'll think about it. Tell me, do you propose to murder Faversham?"

"Faversham will have to go, I'm afraid," said the girl, "but you needn't. And you can't help to save him. If you managed it once you wouldn't twice."

"You lack a certain faith in my ability," mourned Dawlish.

There was no answer, and for a moment Dawlish thought they had been cut off, or else that the girl had hung up. But she spoke again a moment later, and her voice was like a sigh.

"I was afraid so," she said. "Good-bye."

It was conversation that affected Patrick Dawlish oddly. The girl was someone he must have seen several times—perhaps a hundred times. And someone he had met—or seen—at the Carlton. It *must* be possible to find who it was.

"Trouble?" asked Mr. Wishart Cutter from his side. Dawlish turned round, smiling, for he had been half afraid that something had happened to Cutts, who had been in the East End for a long time that morning. But Cutts was safe and sound, with his sparse hair plastered as carefully as ever over his cranium.

"How did you get on?"

"Blanks all the way. The two men we left on guard saw nothing, and the two who followed the people from the Magpie lost their quarries. A dull morning, in fact. I've been trying to get a line somewhere, but failed. Spent half the morning," added Cutter glumly, "in the Magpie. Loaded with policemen and flatfoots, of course. Beer's flat."

118

"Drunken lout," said Dawlish dispassionately; "I thought it was the bottle you were after. I—— Ah-ha, they come!"

He regarded Cutter as he broke off, and Cutter's face was a study. For Eric was ushering three gentlemen—all big and capable, from their appearance, from the bathroom. Their hands were still tied behind them, but their ankles were free. But their faces . . .

Dawlish's smile disappeared. He scowled, taking the only course he could.

"These are the swine, are they? I'm glad you waited for me, Eric, but you can call the Yard now. Let the dead," added Dawlish mournfully, "bury their dead. What did you say?"

"You" was the smallest of the three men, a perky-looking one with an outsize in foreheads. His eyes were blue and blazing and he spluttered at first, but he recovered himself.

"Dawlish, you'll regret this! You'll be summoned for assault and illegal detention and——"

"Sa-ay," drawled Dawlish, frowning again and eyeing Eric, "What's all this? You said they were the Croaker's men."

"Aren't they?" demanded Eric surprisedly. "Well, sir, seeing as how——"

"I'll Croaker's men you," snarled the man with the big forehead. "Dawlish, I'm taking your man with me."

"Where to?" asked Patrick Dawlish.

"The Yard and then Cannon Row. And before I go I'm searching every corner of this flat. They were my instructions, and if this fool here hadn't—hadn't——"

"What?" asked Dawlish unkindly.

"You know what. I'd have finished hours ago. You'll suffer for this, Dawlish, mark my words. I've never been so manhandled in all my life."

"Let's get this straight. Eric heard about the Croaker's impersonation act. You came here professing to be policemen, and I take it without any warrant cards."

"We had cards before we started. We were robbed."

"What's this?" snapped Dawlish, and the three men who had suffered at Eric's hands saw something of the nature of the man for the first time. "You've no warrants?"

"I tell you we were robbed!"

"Tell that to Trivett," snapped Dawlish. "Eric, phone the Yard, and when someone comes tell them to look after this crowd. Had anything to eat with the beer, Cutts?"

Cutter, it appeared, had slaked his thirst and let his appetite do what it wanted. They lunched off Eric's cold meal, and even offered the three Yard men refreshment. The man with the big forehead refused, but the others accepted and were eating when Detective-Sergeant Munk arrived.

In the next quarter of an hour Munk said many things that were not polite, while the men from the Yard—genuine policemen—ransacked the flat. There was no need for them to try and do it in Dawlish's absence now. But they found nothing, and left the flat still swearing vengeance. Cutter chuckled as the door closed behind them.

"You'll have something to answer for, Eric. What happened to their warrants?"

"I was going to suggest," said Eric pontifically, "that we burn them, sir. I have had some experience in picking pockets, and it's surprising how easy it is to rob a policeman." He took three warrant cards from three wallets that appeared as if by magic from his pocket, handed the wallets to Dawlish, and struck a match to light the cards. Even Dawlish was speechless, and Cutter began to laugh.

But he stopped when Dawlish said:

"Business, Cutts. The girl warned me not to go to Chelmsford. She guessed I'd go. She wants me to go."

"Bit backhanded, isn't it?"

"Reasonable," said Dawlish. "She has a nice voice, but I

don't trust her. Anyhow, I'm going to do what she wants and I'm taking Eric with me. Can you get three or four more of your gymnastic friends?"

"I think I can," said Cutter. "You're sure it's wise?"

"I'm sure we'll find a party waiting for us when we get to Faversham's place," said Dawlish. "With luck we might break through. Game to try?"

And Wishart Cutter, thinking of Sir Jeremy Pinkerton, nodded slowly.

"I'll try suicide again," he said. "But——"

What he was going to say didn't come out, for the telephone rang again, and Eric, as if by magic, had it answered. He glanced at Dawlish.

"Mr. Beresford, sir, for you."

It was Beresford, an excited Beresford who could hardly control his voice. And as the words came Dawlish began to smile until at last Cutter and Eric smiled in sympathy. For Ted's words seemed to mean a lot.

"I've located Joan Fayre, Pat. At *Faversham's* house—a place called Greyshott, three miles out of Chelmsford on the Brentwood road. And there are seven or eight men here—Greet among them!"

19

Greyshott

Edward Beresford replaced the receiver at the Red Calf in Chelmsford High Street, and regarded Tony Rawling with a benign smile. Despite the fact that Joan Fayre was at Faversham's house, he was feeling on top of the world. It had not occurred to him or to Rawling, when they had followed Faversham from London to the house called Greyshott, that there was any possibility of finding the girl.

He had learned by telephone from Dawlish of her disappearance and her father's murder, and he had been cast down. But within five minutes of reaching Greyshott he had seen her. She had been outlined for a moment against a top-floor window, and then dragged away.

They had not been able to send for reinforcements immediately, not wanting to leave the house without surveillance, and reluctant to leave each other. From Chelmsford to Greyshott the road was lonely, and queer things could happen.

Several things had happened to make them glad they had been patient.

Hiding behind a clump of evergreens in the grounds—which were about three acres in extent, mostly covered with shrubs—they had seen two carloads of people arrive at Greyshott. Among them had been Cornelius Greet, the manager of the gambling club in Clarge Street, and others they had not recognized.

The VIP's, Beresford had said, of the Croaker's party.

They had allowed the crowd to settle in before making for Chelmsford. Ted's car had been in a lane a hundred yards from the grounds of Greyshott, and they had reached the Red Calf within eight minutes. It took five to get through to London and phone Dawlish, and five to get back to Greyshott.

From a clump of bushes it was possible to see into one of the ground-floor rooms of the house. When they had left it Faversham had been sitting with Greet and two others. The party was larger when they returned—eight men were sitting in the room with a girl.

Her back was toward Beresford, and he believed she was tied to her chair.

"Three miles on the Brentwood road, which is three miles to the left," said Dawlish. "Five minutes and we'll be there, and then—what's the matter, Cutts?"

"I have," said Cutter with dignity, "a presentiment."

"Have it out; they're painful. And don't start getting pessimistic. There's seven of us——"

"And perhaps a dozen or more of the Croaker's men."

"We've beaten bigger odds."

Cutter nodded and forced a smile. Dawlish felt that he was worried, and that the affair was getting on Cutter's nerves. Well, that wasn't surprising. The whole thing was getting on his, Dawlish's, nerves.

Cutter's gloom had one unfortunate effect.

It made Dawlish uncertain of himself, making him wonder whether he was wise in this. It would have been much easier to have told Ted to get back to London.

Dawlish touched the automatic in his pocket, and felt better. It would have been madness to have come down here without weapons, and all of them were armed. They might be contravening the law, but they also had respect for the Croaker's method.

Charleton had talked about that. Charleton was at Brixton, awaiting his trial—the case had not yet come up before the bench for obvious reasons—a victim of the Croaker. For the hundredth time Dawlish asked himself why the Croaker had shopped Charleton, but it was one of a dozen questions to which there appeared no reasonable answer.

They were getting near to Greyshott and Dawlish held his right hand in his pocket. Almost before he expected it the Daimler drove past the house, standing fifty yards from the road and in grounds which were clear near the building, but filled with shrubs near the fences and walls.

Dawlish felt the almost sinister atmosphere of the place as the Lancia flashed by. It was easy to associate the Croaker with it.

He caught a glimpse of Ted Beresford crouching behind a shrub and waving. He saw nothing of the girl sitting in the top-floor window as he passed; she jumped up immediately and left the room.

There was a bend in the main road, and Dawlish braked as soon as they had turned it. He had been thinking fast and thinking hard, and he had the plan of campaign mapped out.

"Cutts, you and I will do it together, shall we?"

"All right." Cutts still seemed anything but enthusiastic.

"Eric—you stay near the front gate, and post a man at every corner. Stop anyone you don't recognize as one of the party, and shoot to wound, not to kill."

"I understand," said Eric heavily.

Dawlish jumped from the car and Cutter followed with alacrity enough. They forced their way through a gap in the hedge surrounding the house, and almost bumped into Tony Rawling.

"How are things?" asked Dawlish.

"Fine, I fancy." Rawling was cautious as ever. "There's a bundle of them, with Faversham, in the front room. You can see them from here. And there's a girl, who looks tied up. Ted's getting hot under the collar."

"Anyone been in or out?" demanded Dawlish as they made their way, keeping under the cover of the shrubs, toward Beresford.

"We haven't seen anyone else, but we were away for a quarter of an hour telephoning," said Rawling. "Greet's still there —you can see him as well as Faversham."

Something more than a warning ticked through Dawlish's mind as he saw the house against the gray background of the Essex lowlands with the gray mist of evening creeping across the fields. Faversham was talking and, occasionally, smiling. Greet was there too.

"Mendor!" he snapped. "So the doctor is involved. We've got a bunch there, sons, but why?"

"Why do you think?"

"Someone knows you're here," said Dawlish. He explained the telephone conversation with the girl who had a voice like an angel—and who was upstairs again now. "But it's too obvious, Ted. They wouldn't keep in that front room if it was a hole-and-corner meeting."

Beresford scowled.

"Look here, Joan Fayre's there——"

"We still want to be reasonably careful. How many cars have passed while you've been hiding here?"

"A dozen at the outside; the road's very quiet. But listen, that girl——"

"I know she's there," said Dawlish, but he gripped Beresford's shoulder. "My worry is why are they waiting for us? The Croaker—if that girl on the phone is to be believed—wants Faversham. To kill Faversham, as they killed his friends. But Greet and Mendor are there as well, both Croaker's men."

"We don't know they're Croaker's men," protested Cutter; "they might be in the swim with Faversham and the syndicate. Greet almost certainly is."

It was a new idea and a good one, and Dawlish admitted the fact generously. Supposing there were *two* organizations. Supposing the syndicate of five, with its myrmidons, had been a competitive gang with the Croaker's? Supposing the Faversham crowd was here and waiting to be wiped out. . . .

But why, Dawlish demanded again, should they sit in a front room so that the world could see them? There were usually limits to self-advertisement, particularly of a man like Greet, who was wanted by the police. And Dr. Mendor would hardly want to be seen in this company.

"Peculiar," admitted Dawlish, but Beresford was fidgeting. Dawlish was by no means sure, now that he was here, that an attack was the surest means of getting results, but he did not propose to back out now.

"We'll try it," he said. "All of us in a bunch to the front door, and—but wait. Where's the Talbot, Ted?"

"Just up the road."

"Hop along and fetch it," said Dawlish with a chuckle. "We'll go up in style, and they'll probably think that we've only just arrived."

Dawlish took the opportunity in the next three minutes to look for Eric or any of the toughs, but they had hidden themselves well, and he doubted even whether the people in the house—if they had seen the four would-be attackers—knew about the ex-boxers. In Eric and his friends Dawlish was pinning a great deal of his faith, and their obvious capability cheered up even Cutter.

Dawlish, Rawling, and Cutter reached the drive as the Talbot drove up. They jumped in and Eric, revealing himself for a few seconds, opened the drive gates. The engine of the Talbot roared toward the front door. Beresford grabbed at the brake, sending it squealing and the tires protesting.

"We won't have to knock, that's one thing," said Dawlish. "I'll do the talking, you keep your hands in your pockets. Ready?"

They were out of the car in a flash, four young men of varying sizes but equal determination. The one idea was to find the Croaker, the one hope to get at the Croaker through this lonely house on the Essex flats. After Dawlish's words none of them spoke, and the only sound, after the echoes of his knock —necessary, after all—had died down, was their heavy breathing.

Then footsteps sounded along the hall, rather short and sharp, and Dawlish wondered whether a woman would open the door. Or a short, jerky man, of the type of Mr. Horatio Fayre, now deceased. His fingers were very tight about the butt of his gun, and all of them stared at the door as it started to move backward.

And then it opened very quickly and they continued to stare. At the incredible. At the machine gun with its ugly snout covering them all, and manned by two gentlemen, brutish-looking, five yards away from the front door, and the little shrewish woman who was sneering at them.

20

Roughhouse

"Good evening," Dawlish said. "Sir Charles Faversham?"

The woman, who was dressed in black and who might have been a layer-out, bared yellow teeth. Dawlish had rarely seen anyone he disliked more.

' 'E's expecting you."

"Mind Percy," said Dawlish, eyeing the machine gun and the gentlemen behind it. "We didn't ask for a civic welcome."

"Cummin!" said the little woman in black. She moved her right hand from beneath her black apron. The gun that showed in her hand was gray. Surprise after surprise was the order of the day, and Dawlish was wondering when he would be able to do his share of reprisals.

Dawlish's voice was shaking.

"Look here, I——"

"If—you—don't—come—in . . ." began the shrew with a voice like sandpaper, "you'll get what you're asking for standing there. See? Come—in!"

Dawlish drew a deep breath and moved forward. He had his right hand in his pocket, still about his gun. He looked past the woman and fired through his pocket, twice in quick succession.

The two men by the machine gun looked pained and then swore, while Dawlish jumped forward, sweeping the startled woman aside with a blow that would have staggered an elephant. He reached the machine gun before either of the gunners recovered from the shock of their wounds, and sent one man flying with a right to the chin and the second by lashing at his knees with his left foot. It was over in a second, and the four men were inside the hall, Rawling at the machine gun and Cutter with him, Beresford at the foot of the stairs, and Dawlish by the door that led to the right—the door that led to the room where the meeting was being held.

Dawlish kicked open the door and jumped in. There was no finesse about his methods, but they had worked more than once and he was prepared to keep backing them. He had a gun in each hand as he stood there, surveying the crowd, with that half-grin on his face and his blond hair awry. He was the blond Atlas again, vast, towering, formidable.

The seven men and the girl round the big table in the room stared in stupefaction, and the only hint of pleasure was in the eyes of the girl. Joan Fayre, with her arms fastened behind her to a stiff-backed chair, leaned forward with her eyes glistening and a prayer in her heart.

The men were like graven images. Faversham had been in the middle of a word and his mouth was gaping open, a caricature of dignity. Greet had pushed his chair back and his right hand was halfway to his pocket, but only halfway. Mendor, the slim, dark doctor, was ashen-faced.

Dawlish recognized none of the others, although he knew he had seen them at the Greet Club on the night of the raid. He waited, breathing hard. It was Faversham who broke the silence in a voice that was more a scrape than anything else.

"Dawl-ish! What does this mean?"

"It means I've come to join the party," said Dawlish cheerfully. "Ted—come in, there's a job for you. Miss Fayre, you'll be all right. Is this your usual method of entertaining visitors, Faversham? If you've harmed Miss Fayre you'll die painfully. Out of your seats all of you, and face the wall."

There was a scraping of chairs as they all obeyed without protest. Faversham's lips were gaping still, and Greet was shivering. The others, with the exception of Mendor, looked scared out of their lives; but there was courage in the doctor who had once been the Guildford police surgeon, although he did not speak. Dawlish singled him out for treatment first, and the treatment was simple.

Beresford came in when he saw Joan Fayre. He was cutting the cords about her wrist when Dawlish's gun butt caught Mendor behind the ear. The doctor collapsed with a grunt, and the others followed in quick succession.

"Why didn't you keep 'em awake to talk?" grumbled Cutter, his cavernous voice like a dirge.

"Time for that," said Dawlish. "Slip out and fetch Eric, will you?"

Wishart Cutter obeyed. He appeared more cheerful, although when he thought of the machine gun his heart bumped unpleasantly. Cutter loved using his fists, but there were limits, and he had no reason to believe that the men behind the machine gun would have treated him gently. Dawlish bellowed after Cutter, "Get them all—and the other car!"

"Ri-ight!" bawled Cutter, and Eric began to hurry toward the front of the house, guessing he was wanted. Ted Beresford was bending over the girl, who was unconscious now, but Dawlish jerked him up.

"Love scenes later, Ted. Carry these men to the Talbot and cart 'em into the road. Then come back for more. Eric"—the ex-bruiser was in the hall now, blowing hard from unusual exertion—"lend Mr. Beresford a hand. Tony, we're going for a walk."

"What's the panic?" asked Beresford, for Dawlish was on tenterhooks.

"I don't know," said Dawlish, "but I want to look round and I want to get out of this place as soon as I can. Keep an eye on that gun before Cutts gets back."

He was in the hall as he spoke, glancing along the drive to Cutter, who was hurrying on after giving the message to the other friends of Eric. One moment he was in his stride, the next he was swaying—swaying—swaying.

He hit the ground with a thud, and dust came up from the dry gravel. In the hall Dawlish and Tony Rawling stood dead still, and Ted's urgent call came again:

"What is it?"

"The—devil!" growled Dawlish, white to the lips. "Cutts was fired at from the house. He fell forward. Someone upstairs —the lot of you, hurry!"

He was galvanized into action, and started to race pell-mell up the stairs, carrying two automatics. Rawling was on his tail, Beresford after him. Eric found a gun from somewhere, and was standing at the foot of the hall, very stolid and wide awake. The footsteps thudded through the house as Dawlish reached the first landing.

And then he stopped.

She was coming from one of the rooms to the left, a small slip of a girl, incredibly lovely. Not beautiful, just lovely. Even in those mad circumstances Dawlish thought of her as adorable. She was holding a pearl-handled automatic in her hand, and she was smiling. So much that she looked as if she would burst into laughter at any moment.

"So we are to meet, Mr. Dawlish."

"*You!*" said Dawlish, and the word was a sigh.

"Yes, you've guessed. I hope I'm as good as you expected although I can't afford to waste time at the moment. I'm sorry I had to shoot Cutter, but I don't like him as much as the rest of you. That bald head, I expect."

Dawlish stopped still, both guns leveled. He had told himself a moment before that he would find it a hard job to shoot this creature, but he changed his mind.

"Ye—es, that's probably it. I won't be sorry to shoot you."

"You won't shoot me," said the girl with the angel's voice. "At least, I shall be surprised if you do. And please don't get histrionics; they always worry me."

"Do they?" asked Dawlish heavily. "That's a shame. You're going to find a lot of other things worry you. How many more of the Croaker's hirelings on the premises?"

"There were two downstairs with the machine gun," said the girl gently. "I'll have to admit that you managed to outwit them—you were quicker than I expected."

"I'm unexpected in a lot of ways. Drop that gun."

The girl laughed and dropped the gun. She was the most self-possessed creature Dawlish had ever met, and he wanted to wring her neck. But he could not deny the fact that she worried him. No one could bluff like that unless she had something up her sleeve.

"Turn round," he growled.

"I'm sorry," said the girl softly. "I can't do everything, Mr. Dawlish. If you've heard any talk of Morelli you'll know that she doesn't do what she doesn't want to do."

"Mor-elli! So you *are* the Speaker!"

"I am the Speaker. And when you questioned me on the telephone the other day you gave yourself away. Brenner forgot to warn you that Morelli was a woman, but that didn't worry me much, or save Brenner. You're foolish, Dawlish," she added dispassionately, and her manner was gradually changing.

"Why?"

"Because you don't know what you're up against. Because you think you can beat the Croaker. Because—well, because you wouldn't take an honest warning when you had it. I don't want to see you dead, but it can't be helped. I tried—with the Croaker's permission—to save you. You had a chance that no one else has ever had or is likely to have, and you threw it away. I knew you'd ignore my warning this morning, I knew you'd come, and now I'm carrying out orders. Do you know why they call me the Speaker, Dawlish?"

"I don't," said Dawlish, and his lips were dry.

"I speak for the Croaker. He rarely talks himself. I give the orders and see that they're carried out. In case you think I'm not capable of it because I'm a woman, I'll tell you some things. *I* shot Pelisse, and his wife knew nothing about it, although she would think it was that fool of a lover of hers."

"You know a lot of fools," murmured Dawlish.

"There are so many about," said the woman. "Well, I shot Pelisse. And that little man you nearly caught, named Deacon. And two Members of Parliament in their flat today. People don't expect these things of a woman."

Dawlish flung out his hand toward her.

She drew back with a gesture that was almost of contempt, and now she was no longer sweet and adorable to look at, but she had the arrogance of a Cleopatra and the cruelty, in her green-gray eyes, of a Borgia. Her lips curled back, too; it was a horrible transformation, but there seemed something hypnotic about it. Three men facing a slip of a girl, and hopelessly outclassed.

"Not so brave, Dawlish? You're wise after all. Look——"

She pointed behind him, but he did not turn round. Instead:

"What is it, Ted?"

Ted Beresford turned and looked—and gasped. Tony Rawling swore, and muttered:

"Dozens of them. God—we can't get through!"

"There never was a chance," said the woman who called herself Morelli. "It isn't often the Croaker brings all his men

133

together, but they're here tonight. To finish you and Faversham, and to have a clean sheet. They were hiding in the shrubs, like your friends, but they're more expert at it."

Dawlish half turned, saw what was happening, and his heart was sick. For *dozens* of men were converging on the house, three or four of them already in the hall, where Eric was slumped on the bottom stair, blood coming from his forehead.

Dawlish's voice cracked.

"The Croaker's men?"

"The Croaker's men. Move out of my path."

She was imperious, arrogant, and there was an overwhelming temptation in Dawlish's mind to obey, simply because she commanded. But he stopped himself in time, and his smile matched hers for grimness when he saw she had a second gun.

"This is where you've made a big mistake, Sister Morelli. Hostages are sometimes useful, and you're one now. No you don't!"

She touched the trigger of her gun, but he was near enough to strike her hand downward. He caught her in a great bear hug as she tried to rush past, and then swung round to face the men who were crowded in the hall.

"Get me—get the Croaker," he said gently, "and take my advice not to shoot."

But five guns in five steady hands were trained upward, and the silence seemed to hum.

21

Roundup

Dawlish had had little time for thinking in the past five minutes, but what he had done had been more than justified. He had felt keenly that there was need for getting away from Greyshott, for a simple single reason: that Faversham and the Croaker led different parties, and that the Croaker would soon arrive.

Why the men at the machine gun were the Croaker's men and not Faversham's he did not know, and for the moment it was useless to try to find out. Nor could he understand how the woman Morelli could roam about Faversham's place at will. Perhaps because Faversham believed she was with him.

They were in a bad spot and Dawlish knew it. There was Eric, still crumpled on the bottom stair and looking a mess; it seemed unlikely that he would ever open his eyes again, for the wound in the side of his head was deep. There were five men of the Croaker's party, bundled together but showing guns in that grim, menacing fashion that seemed part and parcel of the Croaker. There also was the fact that Cutts was still a crumpled heap on the drive—how Dawlish wished he had not been disgruntled with the bald-headed man!—and Eric's four companions were doubtless *hors de combat*. The fact that the Croaker's men had been outside, hiding and waiting, did not really come as a surprise. Dawlish had a feeling that he had half expected it, and he had certainly not been convinced that the attack would end in easy triumph.

Through the windows let into the landing walls and the wall that ran alongside the staircase, and the windows of the rooms, Dawlish saw the Croaker's men walking casually from the border of shrubs and bushes, but all with their hands in their pockets. Apart from the outstretched body of Cutts—*was* he dead?—there was nothing to suggest anything amiss. Even as that thought flashed through Dawlish's mind he saw two men go to Cutter and pick him up. They carried him toward the house. In the hall and at the top of the stairs the tension increased, and Dawlish was hugging Sister Morelli as though he wanted her more than anything else on earth.

And in some ways he did.

Her slim body was as rigid as a poker. She was facing the men in the hall, but Dawlish could see her profile and knew the only expression on her face was one of disdain. Disdain, in these circumstances! She said nothing and they waited, and although it was only for a few seconds, ten at the most, it seemed an age since Dawlish's words had dropped out and the silence had fallen, brooding and ominous.

Dawlish's lips were set and he was no longer smiling. Behind him Beresford was muttering under his breath. Rawling showed no emotion, but he rarely did.

They were waiting; the men in the hall for a word of command from the woman: that much was certain.

Dawlish spoke again, steadily, gently.

"Thinking better of it? You're wise. Miss Morelli—you're in a spot. Supposing you tell them to turn round?"

The woman laughed, but there was nothing angelic about the laughter.

"There are thirty men in or near the house, Dawlish——"

"And three men here with guns," said Dawlish. "You keep

underestimating me. You don't seem to realize that with Cutter as he is and Eric as he is, I'm mad. In a raging way. I would gladly cut your throat, and I probably will before the day's over. Ted——"

"Yes?" Ted Beresford had stopped muttering.

Dawlish kept the muzzle of his gun poking into the woman's side as he whispered:

"Make a dive for the nearest room. Get a chair or something heavy and——"

"Oke," said Beresford, and he dived on the word.

As he moved there was a sudden stab of flame from downstairs and a bullet hummed upward. It missed Beresford by a fraction of an inch. Rawling kept wisely behind Dawlish, and Dawlish behind the woman.

"Tell them to turn round," Beresford repeated softly.

"I tell you you're mad. In five minutes you'll be dead, and——"

"You and the Croaker laughing, eh? I'm disappointed in you in more ways than one. You haven't seen the Dawlish clan in action yet, but you're going to soon. Don't make the mistake of signaling to your friends below, or I'll touch this trigger."

He broke off as, out of the corner of his eye, he saw Beresford coming slowly, cautiously from the room on the left. Beresford could hold a sizable chair like a kitten, and the chair he was holding now was of the fireside variety, heavy but not bulky. It came in sight of the men below before Beresford, and although they started firing as the legs hove into view, they didn't have a chance, for Beresford hurled it downward.

There was a bellow, a grunt, and a crash as the chair landed. Two of the five men went flying and the other three ducked for cover, while as they went Dawlish started shooting. The bullets stabbed out and he found two moving targets. As

137

he fired he moved to the room from which Beresford had come, and hurled the girl into it. She came up with a bang against the opposite wall. Beresford emptied a second gun into the startled crowd below.

Rawling was firing slowly, carefully.

"What's the idea, Pat?"

"To get into that room and barricade it," said Dawlish. "There's no other way. We might be able to last out until something comes or something happens—after all, cars *do* pass this road, and we may raise an alarm."

"Why not run for it now?"

"Against three dozen of them?"

Rawling grinned. The three of them were inside the room now, with the woman Morelli still lying on the floor. But she was conscious, and her eyes were pools of venom. Dawlish ignored her. A wardrobe was hauled against the door—which opened inward—and reinforced by a couple of heavy chairs, and as the last was pushed into position the first thud came against the door.

"They're starting," said Dawlish, his smile tight-lipped. "Ted, watch the window."

Beresford stepped toward it, approaching from the side and looking out.

"I wish Joan were here," he muttered.

"She'll be all right," said Dawlish, although he was by no means sure that he was speaking the truth. "Faversham wanted her, probably to get some information. The Croaker will be on her side."

"Meaning she knows the Croaker?" Beresford was sharp.

"Meaning my tin hat!" blared Dawlish, his nerves suddenly on edge. "Don't be a fool, Ted, get on with the job. Odds aren't easy, are they?"

Beresford's lips tightened, and then he grinned.

"Sorry, Pat. Half a dozen johnnies outside here."

"Near the house?"

"Fifty yards."

Dawlish sidled to the window, the smile back in his eyes. He was wishing that he had more guns in his pockets or more bullets in his guns—it didn't matter much which. But he hadn't. Theirs could be no more than a passive resistance after the first few shots.

He saw the six men approaching.

They were in a semicircle, less than fifty yards away from the window, obviously stalking the room. No one else was in sight, and the sextet was crouching low behind the bushes, although they were plainly visible from the first-floor room. All the time a rhythmic thudding was coming on the door outside, showing that the Croaker's men were busy, working in their inevitable menacing, methodical way.

Ruthlessly. Dawlish thought of the word, and could not keep back a shudder.

"How many bullets left?" His voice was staccato.

"Five in all."

"I've three. Tony?"

"A gunful."

"That makes fourteen," said Dawlish gently. He nodded toward the girl, "You're not carrying a spare gun by any chance?"

Morelli was lying on the floor, but in a more comfortable position now. Her expression was contemptuous, and there was a regal air about her which was hard to resist.

She didn't answer, and Dawlish stepped to her quickly.

"Yes or no?"

Dawlish made no bones about finding whether she had a gun. She had, in the top of her stocking.

"Reinforcements to make sure there are no ladders?" he said gently. "You're thorough, my dear. I—what's *this?*"

"This" was something small but hard in the same

139

receptacle. He took it out, and all the time she was absolutely motionless. But as he glanced down at the little phial of tablets in his hand she made a sudden desperate grab at them, and her eyes were flaming.

"You —— !"

"I should never have thought a voice like yours could pronounce the word," said Dawlish gravely. "Poison, eh? 'I will not be caught alive,' said the Speaker, but she's wrong. You'll be caught alive, and then you'll be hanged."

He put the tablets in his vest pocket, knowing what they were and marveling at the fact that she had them. It told him that the Croaker—and perhaps others who were at the head of the whole organization—did not propose to be caught alive.

"Ted, pick those men off out there, and don't care where you shoot 'em. How close now?"

"Twenty-five yards," said Beresford. He pressed against the wall, poising his gun and poking it through the open window. Morelli gasped as he touched the trigger—the first sign of emotion she had revealed, and Dawlish's lips twisted as he saw one of the six men throw up his arms.

But another, running from the shrubs behind, took his place. Beresford fired again, missed, and tried a third. He found a billet this time, but the man's place was filled again, and the six men came remorselessly onward, their pace never slackening. At the same time the thudding on the door grew more heavy, the wardrobe creaked and groaned and swayed perilously inward. The three imprisoned men were silent, for death seemed to be coming in this last roundup; they had less than twenty bullets between them, and there were thirty men or more ready for the attack.

It did not occur to Dawlish that this was crazy, virtually an open battle near the main road. He didn't know, either, that the road was picketed with "repair" signs, and the Croaker's men were redirecting traffic. He thought of nothing but the fight that was on and its slow, remorseless progress.

And the door opened a fraction of an inch at last, letting a bullet bite into the wall inches from Dawlish's head. There were only minutes left.

22

Odds Overwhelming

"Sons," said Pat Dawlish as the plaster sprayed from the wall, "we're for it. Morelli, move away from that bed. Ted, lend a hand; we'll die fighting."

"Making a break for it?" asked Rawling.

"Not a hope. We'll shove the bed on end across one corner and get behind it. We'll take Morelli with us, and they may hold off, on our terms." He spoke as Beresford grabbed one end of the big double bed in the room, and he took the other. They handled it easily, swinging it across one corner of the room so that it was a foot away from the wall at either end. From the left they could see the window and were able to look through, seeing also the men approaching from outside. Any moment now they expected to see a face at the window or else a bullet coming into the room.

The door was being pushed open inch by inch, the wardrobe was shaking, and the chairs were useless now. Dawlish piled the rest of the furniture in front of the bed, then slipped his tie from his collar.

"Hands behind you, sister."

Morelli was as quiet as ever, but Dawlish acted as if there was no danger, as if the shooting was fanciful and there was nothing on his mind. Tony Rawling kept smiling to himself, while Beresford's chief worry was the girl downstairs. They had a remarkable coolness, these three young men, and the woman Morelli knew that they were not afraid of death.

Dawlish tied her wrists securely with his necktie and guided her behind the bed barricade. As he did so the first bullet cracked through the window and glass scattered in a dozen directions.

Dawlish glanced out, still keeping close to the wall.

There were the six men below, but others were near at hand now. As he looked a speckle of red flame came suddenly and a second bullet cracked into the glass. There was no fear of them being hit from that angle; the Croaker was simply showing his strength. A third came, and a fourth. . . .

"What are they up to?" Beresford's voice was almost casual. With Rawling he was heaving against the wardrobe, but the pressure from the other side was remorseless.

"Running up a ladder," said Dawlish slowly. "They mean to get us. And they're probably worried about Morelli."

"Throw her out to them," suggested Beresford gently.

Dawlish glanced at the woman, and saw the way her breath quickened. Her lips were moving and her breast heaving; she was frightened now, but doing her best not to show it.

Dawlish's expression was dark.

"We'll wait for that, but unless they let up she's in for a nasty time. A very nasty time," added Dawlish, although he doubted whether he could do more than shoot the woman in cold blood. That would be bad enough, but he was convinced the world would be a better place without Morelli. "Lend Tony a hand, Ted. Seconds might help us."

He was watching the crowd below carefully and he could see their heads. But for the scarcity of bullets he would have scattered lead down there; but the bullets would be wanted for the last desperate fight. Was it possible that in five minutes, or a little more, that fight would be over?

Three men against thirty; there wasn't any doubt which way it would end. Well, it would be a minor triumph to take Morelli with them, and as many of the Croaker's men as he could. It was a pity that he didn't know who the Croaker was. Had he known he might have tried a sortie to get the name to the police.

The ladder was coming up, one of the extension type. Two of them. He watched the top of one swaying, and then heard it tap against the windowsill. He saw a chance of doing damage, but as the thought came into his mind the top of the ladder dropped from sight; it was resting against the wall.

No chance of toppling it down, then. At least, no chance without taking a risk.

The tension grew. There was silence broken only by that odd, rhythmic thudding at the door, the creaking of the wardrobe, and the heavy breathing of Beresford and Rawling as they leaned their weight against the barricade and the pressure from the landing. Morelli was in the corner behind the bed.

Dawlish had little doubt that dynamite or fire would have been used by now but for the prisoner. The Croaker's men had no desire to kill the Speaker, and their methods were mild because of it.

Ah! The ladders were in position, men were crawling up them now. Two to each ladder. Dawlish could just see them leave the ground, and his gun was leveled. But as they came higher they went out of his line of vision, and he could only get at them by showing himself.

He showed just his gun, and two bullets spat upward. He tightened his lips and grabbed one of the chairs from the barricade at the door.

He hoisted the chair to the windowsill and tipped it over. As it went he leaned out, outlined for a moment against the side of the house and grabbed the tops of the ladders. He heaved

144

them sideways with the bullets flying, mostly stopped by the chair. Like a scene from a slow-motion film he saw the ladders toppling backward, the men clinging to them like ants. He saw the chair crash down, taking one man with it, and saw the others spreading out to get away from the danger. The ladders crashed and the men with them, but a spatter of bullets pecked into the window and the wall. Dawlish felt a stinging pain in the back of his hand, and saw the gash of a bullet wound.

But he was smiling, and he even winked at Morelli, for the Croaker's men were back where they had started.

"You're a fool," she said. "You haven't a chance."

"Ten minutes ago I hadn't a chance of living for five minutes. You could settle the problem, couldn't you?"

"How?"

"Giving orders. Unless the Croaker is here."

"Never mind the Croaker. What orders?"

"Tell them to give us a free passage, and we'll give you yours." Dawlish was smiling but he did not seriously think she would do it. In fact, he was sure, and he was right.

"The orders for today are that you and your friends mustn't get away."

"So the Croaker would rather see me dead than you alive?"

"Yes."

"And what do you think about it?"

"It's a pity, but there was always the possibility. I suppose you'll shoot me?"

"Sad though it seems, yes. My contribution to the Croaker's downfall."

"My death won't seriously worry him."

"He'll have to find another Speaker."

"He might speak for himself," said Morelli ominously. "He hasn't much farther to go now, Dawlish. We're nearly at the end of the run."

"*Are* you, by Jove! A pity Trivett doesn't know that."

"Trivett will probably never know, because he has annoyed the Croaker."

"Just as I did, eh?" Dawlish's smile, that half-inane smile. He glanced out of the window every few seconds, and he saw that the ladders were coming up again, while the pressure at the door was almost too great for Beresford and Tony Rawling to withstand. There was a six-inch gap, and soon a man would be able to squeeze through.

And then the bullets would start flying until they were spent, and——

"So you're not afraid of death? It's a pity, because that bargain sounded good to me."

"No, I'm not afraid. And I can't strike bargains. The Croaker *is* here."

"Is he, by God!" Dawlish's lips tightened, and the power of the blond man revealed itself now. "So the Croaker came in person. He wasn't with Faversham's crowd?"

"You're thinking of Greet or Mendor. No, neither of them. You'll never know who the Croaker is, Dawlish."

"Seeing that I'm booked for the nether regions, what harm could it do?"

Morelli shrugged. Her voice *was* angelic now, and so was her expression. It seemed incredible that this adorable-looking little person could act as she, could admit to half a dozen murders and worse.

"I've sworn never to name the Croaker, and I'm the only one who can."

"You stick to all your bargains like that?"

"Have you ever known me anything but honest?" asked Morelli. "Oh, I don't mean with money. Money's communal property anyhow and no man has a right to as much as Fayre had, for instance. I'm not worried about money. I'm just working for the Croaker."

146

Dawlish's eyes were gleaming.

"Fond of him, eh?"

"Very," said Morelli, and she seemed to sigh. "But *have* you ever known me lie?"

Dawlish looked at her without speaking. As he did so he saw the men mounting the ladder again and he prepared for another effort.

"No, I haven't. It's going to be hard to put a bullet through you, but I'll make sure you're out in one."

"Thanks." She was laughing now, and he could see the gleam in her eyes. Dawlish sidled to the window again, grabbed a chair and poised it——

Then he stared.

For something was happening down there. Panic. Men running *away* from the house, cries that could only be of alarm and perhaps fear. Suddenly, the blazing of rifle and revolver shots from the shrubs, the flashes of yellow flame and a menacing cordon approaching the house. *Approaching the house!* An attacking party.

The—police!

23

Some Satisfaction

It hardly seemed possible at first, and the word went through Dawlish's mind a dozen times. The police, *police,* and armed at that.

He saw their helmets, dozens—hundreds!—of helmets, and he saw the cordon advancing as slowly and as grimly as ever the Croaker's men had come. There was no time for thinking, only time for a tremendous exhilaration. The police were here!

His eyes were flashing as he swung round.

"Ted—Tony—ease off! Trivett's men, and we're safe for a pension. Sister, your luck's deserted you."

Morelli's face had changed, and it was like alabaster. Could this arrogant-looking shrew be the girl he had talked to three minutes before? Dawlish didn't think so, but he was too relieved to worry much.

Beresford grunted, Rawling laughed. None of them was entirely free from an exuberance that was close to hysteria. Morelli was silent and deathly white, standing against the corner with her eyes turned toward the window.

The thudding on the door had ceased, men were shouting outside and footsteps thudding against the stairs. Panic was in the Croaker's men and—the Croaker was here!

Dawlish's eyes were blazing.

"It's lucky you didn't name the Croaker, he might have had

a shock. It looks as though you might have some third degree, too."

He broke off as he saw the thing happening, and he was standing by the window with the others, staring out. From the front of the house the car appeared—Ted's Talbot, as it happened—with three men in it, and a machine gun.

The gun from downstairs.

It was blazing away and the flames from its ugly snout seemed like a perpetual catherine wheel. The engine roared, the Talbot hewed its way through men and bushes toward the road. All the time the *tap-tap-tap* of the machine gun was clearly audible and the deeper sound of the rifles and revolvers that the police were using.

Could the car get away?

Dawlish believed that the Croaker was in it. The Croaker had seen that the odds had swung against him, that there was little or no chance of his escaping detection at last, unless he escaped altogether. And he was making a most spectacular dash.

No one knew how many police there were, but the total must have reached nearly a hundred. For a lone car to force its way through that cordon seemed impossible; but the driver did not hesitate, and there *was* a chance of escape.

Dawlish watched fascinated. Beresford was biting at his lips, Rawling was smiling, and Morelli—who had managed to reach the window—was smiling more widely.

The car reached the gate and swung through on two wheels, its tires screeching. The roar of the engine was like an airplane in full flight. It turned right, toward Brentwood, and Dawlish could see the policemen in the road dashing for cover as the bullets sprayed out from the machine gun.

And then he saw the car coming in the opposite direction.

He didn't know that Trivett was at the wheel, a Trivett who

was determined that no one should get away from the great roundup, but he could understand the supreme courage of the driver. The two cars raced toward each other, and Dawlish knew that the policeman meant to force a crash.

Head-on, at fifty miles an hour or more. It was horrible, and yet he could not keep his eyes off it. He saw the way the driver of the Talbot was crouching over the wheel, he could see the road was wider where they would meet, and then he saw the Talbot swing to the left, up the bank at the side of the road. The cars flashed past, the police car swerved but missed the other by a fraction of an inch; and then the Talbot went racing along the clear road.

Chief-Inspector William Trivett was a happy man in many ways, and could honestly say that he had derived much satisfaction from the affair at Greyshott. He was not altogether satisfied, for although he had the Speaker, and a dozen or more of the Croaker's men were in prison—with the rest in hospital —the Croaker had escaped.

Dawlish said that he deserved it.

"It took guts, but all he deserves is a noose," Trivett said. "Confound it, I'm inclined to think you're glad he got away."

Dawlish chuckled and pushed his hair back from his forehead.

"Still linking me with the Croaker?"

"After this, how can I?" asked Trivett. "But it's time you told us what happened."

"Your story first," Dawlish insisted; "and while I remember it, I'll admit that I've never been so glad in my life to see a policeman as I was when I caught a glimpse of the first helmet. How *did* you manage to get here?"

Trivett smiled, and lit a cigarette from Dawlish's case.

They were in the room where the mess had been made,

Dawlish and Trivett alone. Rawling had hurried out to try to find Cutter, or what was left of Cutter, and Eric. Beresford was looking for Joan Fayre, and praying that she was safe. The police were tidying up the mess, and ambulances and Black Marias had been busy for the past half hour.

Trivett had escaped from the car crash—he had overturned after the Talbot had passed him—with no injuries to worry about, and Sergeant Munk had already registered his approval. So had the Assistant Commissioner of Scotland Yard and the Chief Constable of Essex; both had watched the fight from a distance.

And now Trivett was talking.

"You'll remember I told you that you were being followed?"

"Yes; and so was Faversham."

"Yes. We had the report from Faversham's trailers that he was at Greyshott, and a little later word from Munk—who was on your tail—that you were here. He found a café on a slight rise a mile away, and watched you from there. When the shooting started he called the Yard and the Essex headquarters, and we didn't lose much time. I don't think squad cars have ever traveled so fast. I'm sure I never have."

"What made you bring such a strong force?"

"Munk. He can be insistent, and he was using powerful glasses. He glimpsed the hall of Greyshott when you went in, and he spotted the machine gun. When we learned that was in the offing we didn't take many chances. In another half hour you would have had a battalion of the Essex Guards on hand, tanks and machine guns and all."

Dawlish blew smoke toward the ceiling.

"You didn't propose to take any chances, Trivett."

"Why should we? We wanted to get the Croaker badly, and we knew what kind of fight he would put up. My one regret," added Bill Trivett a little glumly, "is that we didn't get the Croaker."

"Are all policemen greedy?" demanded Dawlish, and before Trivett could make the obvious retort he plunged into a recital of the affairs at Greyshott, including the fact that Faversham, Mendor, and Greet—with the four members of the syndicate—had run an organization in opposition to the Croaker's.

"You don't know what kind of organization?" Trivett asked.

"Only that it was crooked, and the Croaker didn't like it. Or he wanted its fruits for himself. The Croaker has earned the other name of Poacher very well, Bill. He could never be satisfied with what he earned himself. However, you've got Faversham, haven't you?"

Trivett's eyes lighted up.

"Yes." He turned abruptly toward the door. "Well, I'd better be looking round. Coming?"

"I am," said Dawlish.

He was conscious of an odd feeling, almost as if he was still dreaming. Not for a moment had he thought that there would be any chance of an escape, and the world seemed unreal. So did the story Trivett had told, although it was natural enough.

Dawlish did not know yet whether Cutter, or Eric, or Joan Fayre were alive. He didn't know whether Joan knew anything about the Croaker, or why she had been kidnapped, and he considered that would be worth learning. And there were other things.

The daze which had filled his mind for the past half hour was gone, and he hurried down the stairs decisively. He smiled to himself when he remembered what had happened there, and saw the wreck of the chair that Beresford had hurled on the men massed in the hall. When he looked at the affair properly there was a lot to laugh about in it.

152

But there was nothing to laugh about with Eric.

The bullet had not pierced the brain, but it had gone perilously close to it. He was being put in an ambulance when Dawlish reached the drive, and the blond young man uttered a prayer; Eric had given more than good service.

And there was Cutter.

Dawlish remembered his friend's reluctance, and that phrase: "I'll try suicide again." Cutts *had* had a presentiment and it seemed as though it had been well justified. Dawlish felt that he would never forgive himself if Cutts' injuries proved fatal.

He banged into Beresford a moment later.

"How's your Joan?" Dawlish spoke automatically.

"Indoors taking nourishment! I came to help clear up. Seen Cutts yet?"

"No. I wish I had."

The beam lost itself from Beresford's face, and they hurried along the drive to the place where Cutter had been lying when they had last seen him. Dawlish was telling himself that he had been lying right in the path of the racing Talbot, and——

There was no sign of spilt blood. They turned right, and out of the gloom—for dusk was falling now—loomed the bucolic figure of Detective-Sergeant Munk of Scotland Yard. Munk was smiling, a rare thing for him.

"Howdo, folk? All OK, then?"

"Thanks to a police sergeant, I'm told," said Dawlish, and he extended his hand. Munk's grip was very firm.

"Glad to be of service, gents, but don't go pushing *me* in a bathroom next time I call. Was you looking for anything?"

"Yes—Mr. Cutter."

"Ain't seen a sign, but we haven't looked in them bushes near the gate yet. Coming?"

There was no sign of Cutter, and he was finding it hard to understand. He would have given a great deal to be sure the bald-headed man wasn't lying dead somewhere, and . . .

"Looking for something?" asked Mr. Cutter genially, and he loomed—as Munk had loomed—out of the gathering dusk. He was bedraggled, and there was a nasty wound in his fore-head and a scratch in his neck. Dawlish and Beresford fell on him until Cutter called for peace.

"Where'd you get to?" Dawlish asked as they strolled back toward Greyshott. "We thought——"

"Which just proves you shouldn't think," said Cutts. "I've been busy. Trying to find Eric's four friends."

It came to Pat Dawlish very suddenly that he had not given a second's thought to the four men from the gymnasium, and his conscience smote him. But Cutter's news was good. None of them was badly hurt.

"And so," said Dawlish, as they stepped into the hall and saw Trivett talking to two distinguished-looking gentlemen, "all we want now is the Croaker. *And* we'll get him."

"It's past time you did," snapped a little man with a voice that started on bass and quavered up to falsetto. "I'm ashamed of you, Pat. How are you, my boy?"

And Sir Jeremy Pinkerton, seventy, gray, and smiling, stepped from the room on the right with his hand extended.

24

Faversham Talks

Dawlish said afterward that he too tired for fresh shocks, and that what he really needed was a long night's sleep. He simply stared at his uncle, and for a moment forgot to extend his hand. But he remembered himself at last, while Pinkerton chuckled in that up-and-down way of his.

"Surprised to see me, Pat? Not unexpected, after all. I was getting a bit worried about you, and I came up to London this morning. Was with Archie when the call came through from that Munk fellow, and here I am. How are you?"

"Dazed, hungry, thirsty, and delighted," said Dawlish. "So you're getting really fond of me."

"None of that, none of that," snapped Pinkerton, but his rheumy old eyes were twinkling. "Archie—do you know Pat? My nephew. The man Dawlish you've been so worried about."

One of the distinguished-looking gentlemen turned with a half-smile, and Dawlish shook hands with the Assistant Commissioner of Scotland Yard—the man who was in charge of the Croaker case. Sir Archibald Morely was young for his job, and a pleasant-looking man whom Dawlish had often seen but never officially met. Morely, he realized, would be the man who had ordered Trivett and others to keep a watchful eye on him.

Moreley's handshake was firm and his voice pleasant. Dawlish liked the expression in his eyes.

"Yes. I'm the guilty party, and you asked for it. But after today's show I haven't the heart to reprimand you."

"Which shows a nice feeling," said Dawlish with his lazy smile. "The Croaker will want his own back, and, much more important, he'll want the Speaker."

"You mean Miss Morelli?"

"We're getting formal," riposted Dawlish. "Yes, I mean Morelli. There's a stronger link between her and the Croaker than we imagined. However, we can't do much more here. Or are you going to get Faversham to talk before you take him back to London?"

Sir Archibald Morely shook his head.

"No, I don't think it's wise. He's on the way to the Yard now, anyhow, and we're going back in a matter of minutes. Coming?"

"Am I allowed at the séance?"

"In the circumstances, I think yes."

"I'll be there," said Dawlish cheerfully, "but I'll come back with my party and see you at the Yard."

Dawlish went farther into the house, to find Ted Beresford sitting on the edge of a couch and looking at Joan Fayre with eyes that said a great deal. It was really remarkable how Beresford had fallen for a girl he had known only for a few hours.

But—there was the news of her father's death to come.

He learned from Beresford that she knew nothing of it, and left it to him to break the news. Ted said, ten minutes later, that she took it well, but she was more than upset. On the other hand, there had not been a great deal of sympathy between father and daughter so the shadow of the murder would probably not last for long.

Dawlish was tempted to try to find out why Joan had been kidnapped, but he decided against it for the moment. The police would want to know in due course, and somehow he did not think that she would refuse to talk.

Joan elected to return to London with them in the Daimler.

Eric's four friends were all on the way to Chelmsford for medical treatment, and Cutter had been bandaged by a doctor —one of five called to the house. Ten minutes after the police car had left with Morely, Sir Jeremy Pinkerton—Dawlish was still dazed when he thought of the fact that his uncle had arrived here from Surrey—Trivett and the Essex Chief Constable, Dawlish's Daimler started in their wake.

The Daimler passed the police car ten miles along the road, and reached London half an hour ahead. Time, as Dawlish said, for tea at the flat, and dinner would have to come later.

They missed Eric, but Joan Fayre proved that a millionaire's daughter need not be helpless. Ted continued to beam. Cutter, stiff from his wounds, but more than cheerful now that his presentiment had proved a false guide, chattered a great deal, and Tony Rawling made an occasional weighty remark.

"Joan, what happened last night after the Greet Club raid?" Dawlish asked.

The girl was worried, and showed it. She was still dressed in the maroon-colored evening gown, for she had had no opportunity to change.

She drew a deep breath.

"You want the whole story?"

"Of course."

"We-ell—it's not altogether a nice one. Have you a cigarette, Ted."

Ted lit one for her and she drew reflectively on it before she went on.

When she had finished Dawlish was sure that she had told the truth.

The affair had started two years before, when her father had joined the board of a small company on which were Faversham, the two murdered M.P.'s, and Sir Hugo Pelisse. Until that time Horatio Fayre had been reasonably honest, but the company was a cloak for nefarious activities and the girl learned of it.

She was loyal because of the family tie to her father, but hated the other members of the syndicate. She wanted proof of what they were doing, which was why she visited the Greet Club so often, and why her father was so annoyed to find her there.

"You found the proof?" asked Dawlish.

"Near enough. Yesterday morning. And I was going to threaten Faversham and the others with it. Unless they let Father out of the syndicate I was going to the police. Daddy was strong in some ways," she added with a shiver, "but Greet and Faversham and that dreadful man Mendor were too much for him."

"Taken as read," said Dawlish.

"And so I went to the meeting last night. I was silly enough to let Faversham know what I was thinking of doing, and he managed to get me away from Father. They were spending most of the time at the meeting this afternoon, discussing what they were going to do with me. They stuffed some cotton wool in my ears half the time, to make sure I couldn't hear what they said."

"And you heard nothing?"

"Only a bit about the Croaker, and what they were going to do with him. I think it was bluff. They all seemed scared of the Croaker."

"And small wonder, with the other members dead," said Dawlish gently. "Have you any other relatives?"

"Not in London," admitted Joan Fayre.

"Then you'll have to go to Ted's until this is over, because queer things might happen." Dawlish smiled, and Joan raised

158

no objection. She felt weary and tired and anxious only for a rest, which was understandable.

Beresford took her to his home in St. John's Wood, Cutter and Rawling promised to make sure that Fortnum & Mason did their damnedest for a meal when the others returned, and Dawlish made his way thoughtfully to Scotland Yard.

The affair of Fayre was settled. He believed Joan, and he was later proved justified. She had told the truth, and the nervous manner of Horatio Fayre that morning was caused by fear of what Dawlish knew and dread lest the Croaker, not Faversham, had kidnapped his daughter.

But who had killed Fayre?

Perhaps Faversham, feeling the man could not be trusted because of the girl, had decided to put him out. Faversham's people used the same guns as the Croaker's, and——

Damn it, Mendor *had* shot Fayre.

Dawlish was telling himself he had found the truth when he thought of something else which made him stop dead still. His right foot was inches off a taxi runningboard.

"Where to?"

"Scotland Yard," said Dawlish, and went into the cab very thoughtfully—full of the words which Morelli had uttered. It looked as if she had told at least one lie, for she claimed to have shot Fayre, and Dawlish was sure that nothing in skirts had been near when the millionaire had died.

"Your wisest course, Faversham," said Sir Archibald Morely quietly, "is to tell the whole truth. There is ample evidence from the other members of your company that you have condoned murder on at least one occasion, and quite frankly you will be taken before the courts on a capital charge. If you give us all possible help, both on the matter of your own activities and those of the Croaker as far as you know them, you will have a chance of less than a life sentence. Otherwise that is unavoidable."

Faversham drew a deep breath.

"I'll tell you," he muttered. "I—I was only one of many, Morely. Fayre—Pelisse—they were much more important than I. They gave the orders——"

"We'll work that out afterward," said Morely, and the sting of contempt in his voice made Faversham flush. From then on the baronet talked, and what he said was amazing. Even to Dawlish and the policemen, who knew that these crimes had more than ordinary importance, and who had expected large figures.

They had not expected the millions of the Faversham racket, and they had certainly never dreamed of the thing that the Croaker knew. That in gold bar and precious stones there was a fortune hidden somewhere in or near London, and that the Croaker was after it. It was the proceeds of the Faversham gang crimes, of the gaming club, of a dozen rackets; *and only Sir Hugo Pelisse had known where it was!*

25

Money for Whom?

There was a hush at the room in Scotland Yard where the conference was taking place. Even Faversham stopped talking as he made that last admission.

Sir Archibald Morely looked as though this was a story out of the *Arabian Nights*. Sir Jeremy Pinkerton—who had contrived by reason of his friendship with the A.C. and the Home Secretary to be present—was blinking with his hooded eyes going up and down oddly. Trivett bit his lip, and his cheek muscles were working. The Essex man gasped, and Dawlish took cigarettes from his pocket, making the others jump as he dropped the case onto the table.

"Cigarettes? So what?"

Everyone present took a cigarette and accepted a light without saying a word. The whole prospect seemed so bizarre and yet so convincing that they were temporarily stunned. Dawlish was in better control of his faculties than any of the others, but he knew when to keep quiet, and that this was one of the occasions. His to sit and listen, the others to ask the whys.

Morely tapped his fingers on the polished desk.

"So that's it, is it. And how big is this cache?"

"It—it must be at least two million," muttered Faversham, biting at his cigarette. "Of course, most of the money has been distributed, under the guise of profits of the company that we

161

formed together. But there must be two million at the hiding place."

"Why as much as that?"

"We—Pelisse and the others, that is"—Faversham was doing his damnedest to make sure the dead men took most of the blame, and certainly it would not do them a great deal of harm—"thought it best to have something negotiable ready in case of emergency. Pelisse was our chairman, and he looked after everything."

"You seriously mean you let *one* man control two million pounds?" demanded Morely skeptically.

"No, no, we didn't. We all had information, in code, but it was stolen."

Dawlish felt his stomach quivering and Sir Jeremy said, "Tcha!" The atmosphere of the A.C.'s room tensed.

"By whom?"

"The Croaker—who else would do it?" Faversham was sweating now, but the whole truth was coming, and that meant a great deal. "He shot Pelisse after the notes had been sent round. Pelisse's flat was burgled and his code message—he kept one for himself, of course—was taken. I know, because I visited his flat soon afterwards."

"Didn't Pelisse live at Lanster Place?" demanded Patrick Dawlish.

"Yes, but he also had a flat. For—well, you know the relations between him and his wife. Pelisse wasn't exactly faithful."

"Let's leave those details," said Morely, who was a happily married man. "Where is the flat?"

"181a, Queen's Mansions, Buckingham Palace Road."

"Send a call, Trivett," said Morely, and Trivett stepped to the telephone. "Go on, Faversham."

The baronet dabbed his forehead with a handkerchief that was already damp.

"Fayre was killed for the same reason. I sent a man there soon afterwards, but the note was missing. Fayre always kept it in his safe."

Dawlish whistled, and Trivett, who had finished on the telephone, knew why. But Dawlish was sure there had been no code message among the papers he had taken from Fayre's safe. But he made a suggestion quickly.

"The footman at Fayre's place let me get away with a lot. Was the footman your man, Faversham?"

"No, no!" Faversham meant what he said. "He might be the Croaker's!"

Trivett suggested that they should send for a man to make the necessary telephone calls. He wanted to hear all that there was to hear. Sergeant Munk had just returned to the Yard, and he came in answer to the summons. Munk telephoned to another office, to send men to Fayre's house to try to detain the footman, if he was still on the premises, while Faversham's story went on:

"Golding and Renway were killed together at their flat, and the place must have been ransacked," said Faversham. "I don't know who killed them."

"The Speaker did," Dawlish said. "I mean Morelli. Is she here, Morely?"

"Yes, downstairs. Munk——"

Munk went out to collect Morelli, and for a while a lull fell over the talk. But all of them were thinking the same thing.

The Croaker had killed members of the syndicate of crime, and had taken the code messages. The Croaker, living up to his reputation to the last, had planned to poach on the other gang's preserves. The question was: did he know the code, could he understand why so much money was stacked away?

Munk came in, Morelli with him. She was looking pale and bedraggled, but that startling beauty could not be disguised. Even though she was cold and arrogant now, looking on the gathering as though every member was a long way beneath her, they had to admit that she carried herself with a superb poise. Sir Jeremy jumped to his feet and offered her his chair.

She looked contemptuously at Faversham, who seemed more scared now than he had done before.

"I suppose you've talked," she said.

"He's told us everything he knows," said the A.C. sharply, "and we hope you are going to assist us, Miss Morelli. As I've told Faversham, there is a capital charge awaiting you both, and the only possible escape for you is to turn King's Evidence."

The woman smiled, and for a moment she looked ravishing. That angel's voice was there too.

"I'm not going to turn King's Evidence. I've tried all I know and I've lost, and that's all there is to it."

Dawlish looked, quite accidentally, across the table; and he saw the rheumy eyes of his uncle regarding the girl. Was he regarding her wistfully? He was too old to be affected too much by her beauty and he had never been a ladies' man. Yet . . .

"Don't be a bloody fool," said Dawlish to himself, and he smiled widely. "Well, if you won't talk, you won't. But you've no objection, I take it, to clearing one or two minor mysteries up?"

"Providing they don't affect the Croaker now, no."

"Then, we'll start, and we'll go right back. The Croaker has simply organized crime, poaching on criminals—save the word—and ordering them to work for him—once. He's never used the same man twice unless that man has been a member of the central organization. That much we've reasoned. Right?"

"Right!"

She was laughing at him.

"Good. The Croaker has been working for at least eighteen months——"

"Two years, almost to the day."

"Thank you again. Two years, then. And in that time he's managed to amass a fortune of?"

"Well, two or three millions."

"Fairly satisfactory, seeing the expenses he's had to stand at. Now we're getting a little more particular. Among other places the Croaker had his headquarters at the Magpie, Aldgate High Street?"

"That's right."

"None of the daily staff knew about it?"

"None of them, only that there was someone called the Speaker lodging in one of the upstairs rooms."

"And you were the Speaker—right. Now the other night at the Magpie. Why was Charleton shopped?"

"That's an ugly word," smiled Morelli, and not once did she show the slightest sign of awkwardness or anxiety. "He was running with the hounds, and—I've forgotten the saying, but there it was. He was working for Faversham as well as us."

Every eye was turned to Faversham. Every man present knew that the statement was true, and the general opinion of Superintendent Charleton grew lower.

"How did you find it out?" asked Dawlish.

"Slowly," admitted Miss Morelli. "It started, I think, just after the affair at Sir Jeremy's place in September. Mendor was working for us—you would be surprised, Sir Archie, to know how many policemen and doctors have helped us from time to time—and he helped to arrange the affair. But Charleton wasn't satisfied. You see, no money is paid out unless a job succeeds. That one didn't succeed. Mendor was approached by Fayre—who knew the doctor worked for the Croaker— and Mendor accepted a bribe. He and Charleton started working for Faversham then. Faversham's crowd were worried because the Croaker was too successful, and they felt there wasn't room for two—gangs shall I say?—in England."

165

"And the Croaker didn't think there was room either?"

"He didn't. But he guessed that the Faversham crowd would be putting something aside for a rainy day and he waited until that something was really large before starting to work. As soon as the Croaker learned that Pelisse was controlling the hoard he began to work. I obtained the code messages—you've probably heard about them from Faversham—but unfortunately two are still missing. One that Horatio Fayre had, and I don't know who's got that. And Pelisse's own code. So you see the Croaker has the code covering the money—perhaps only one. But no one, I think, can really read the code, except Faversham."

"And Faversham won't be leaving here," said Morely suddenly.

But he broke off, for Dawlish was on his feet, his eyes gleaming oddly. And Dawlish started to speak:

"So there are two messages missing, eh? Fayre's—which I might have in Fayre's papers or Joan Fayre might have tucked away, and Pelisse's, which his wife might have. Morely, you must find Naida Pelisse."

26

Fayre's Message

Only Morelli seemed really self-possessed after Dawlish's commentary and she was smiling, almost as if she still held something up her sleeve.

Morely spoke at last:

"Munk, get someone working, and send a general call out. Dawlish—what do you mean by 'I might have Fayre's message'?"

Dawlish explained that he had been the first at Fayre's safe. He said simply that he had seen no code, and that he believed Joan Fayre knew nothing of it. On the other hand . . .

"Where are the papers you took from the safe?" Morely was looking at Trivett, and the inspector stood up.

"In my office. I'll get them."

He was back in three minutes, with the sheaf of papers. Dawlish, a trifle easier in his mind, smiled when he saw them. Morely took each one and shook it carefully, to make sure nothing was lodged in it, and as he turned the last sheet— showing the final figures for the profits of the Greet Club— Faversham gasped.

Dawlish looked up quickly.

"What's worrying you?"

"That's it—the figures on the back there! I'm sure because it's identical with the one I had. It——"

And then a thing that seemed impossible happened.

Morelli's expression changed and if the others had been looking at her they would have understood, without a shadow of doubt, the devil that was in her. She leaned forward with an incredibly fast motion toward Dawlish. Dawlish was looking at Faversham and didn't see her, knew nothing until he felt the tug at his pocket. He swung round, but Morelli had his gun. Morelli was aiming at Faversham . . . *Morelli fired!*

And Faversham took the bullet through the temple and fell forward, spattering blood over the table and over Sir Jeremy's hands.

She was standing in the cell, very tight-lipped now, and nearer a natural woman than Dawlish had ever seen her. Morely was there too, with Trivett and Sergeant Munk. Sir Jeremy had gone. All of them were very grim, and Morelli was almost distraught. Her hair was awry, and there were tears in her eyes, but her voice was steady.

"I know, and don't care! Faversham deserved to be dead anyhow. And that money's the Croaker's—he's earned it if any man has! He's going to get it!"

"It will be quite impossible for you to make a defense," Morely said. "You've damned yourself."

"There was proof against me in any case. I've only had one chance since Dawlish took me this afternoon, and that's that the Croaker will get me away. If he can't—well, it isn't worth living. Can you understand that, you fools? I *love* the Croaker. I've made the Croaker what he is. He's mine! And no one else will get him, no one else will ever know his name. Now get out, get out, get out!"

Dawlish gripped her wrist.

"Who is the Croaker?"

"Get away from me, get away! I won't tell you, I won't!"

Dawlish insisted roughly.

"Who *is* the Croaker?"

She stared at him, the tears welling from her eyes now. Dawlish had been questioning her in that same level voice for the past two hours. They did not allow third degree in England, but there were other things, and Dawlish was the only man who seemed to be proof against her wiles. He had worn her down until she was a wreck now, distraught, terrified, *human*. What love she bore the Croaker!

"It's no use, Dawlish. You've tried, but if the Croaker knew what you were doing to me he would kill you. But I won't tell him. I'm fond of you myself."

"Why should the Croaker be fond of me?"

"I don't know. Why am I?"

Dawlish was silenced for a moment, but tried again, tightening his grip on her arm.

"You've done your best, but we *must* know who the Croaker is. If we know who the Croaker is today it might save hundreds of lives. . . ."

"You're talking nonsense and you know it."

She fell forward suddenly in Dawlish's arms, and he knew she was not foxing. She was finished for the time being, and Dawlish looked at Morely with a faint smile.

"I'm not sorry. She'll never give way, Morely."

"I was afraid not," admitted the Assistant Commissioner. "So what now?"

"Nothing until we can trace Pelisse's wife. You've had no luck?"

"None at all."

"You're watching those two addresses I gave you?"

"Of course," said Morely.

"And you're watching Sir Jeremy?"

"Yes."

"I've never known my uncle so concerned about me. 'Get on with it and be damned' is his usual motto. Why did he come from Dorking today?"

"I can't be sure, but he certainly wasn't at Greyshott until I arrived; he was with me all the time."

"I'm talking nonsense, perhaps, but I can't get rid of the idea that there is some definite reason why I'm alive, that the Croaker has got a soft spot for me. It can't be anyone else——"

"It might be a hundred people. You know plenty, and you didn't know Morelli. Did you?"

"No."

"And she's not joking when she says she's fond of you; it's the truth. Anyhow, there will be two men watching your father —sorry—uncle." Morely pushed his hand through his hair. "I'm getting prepared to call my own mother my aunt. Anything else?"

"Joan Fayre's being watched?"

"But she's at the Beresfords'. You're not going to tell me that Beresford——"

"No, no, I'm not going to tell you anything, I'm just on a razor edge and can't get off it. Someone else is working for the Croaker, and the Croaker will get away with that half-million *and* a hundred—more or less—murders unless we're busy. The one good thing is that he can't read the code message. Morelli admitted that. So he can't find the hoard yet."

"He'll probably have a code expert."

"Who might be one of those we finished at Greyshott. Remember the Croaker got away with only a few men."

"That's assuming he was in the car."

"It doesn't mean anything of the kind; it just means that three of the Croaker's men got away in the Talbot and the Croaker *might* have been with them. Otherwise he'll have met them somewhere outside."

170

Morely nodded, and they went from Cannon Row to the Yard. The A.C. dispensed drinks, and Dawlish, with Sergeant Munk to see him most of the way, started for his flat.

Dawlish had been reasonably clear-headed until Morelli had shot Faversham, and from that moment the whole scheme of things had seemed to go crazy. He had never dreamed she would go to such lengths, but she had killed Faversham simply to prevent the police from learning the cipher from which the code message could be transcribed, and thus from robbing the Croaker.

The code was being worked on by the Home Office experts, but it was by no means sure that they would find the solution until after the Croaker had managed it.

Dawlish smiled to himself sardonically, and Sergeant Munk said inaudibly the gent ought to have some sleep, he was getting too tired. Dawlish would have agreed had the sergeant spoken aloud, for he felt that he could stand little more for a while.

Morelli had sacrificed herself for the Croaker, a Croaker who held him, Dawlish, in considerable esteem. *Was* it Sir Jeremy Pinkerton? Could that raid on the Towers have been a blind to hoodwink the police and the others?

In his cooler moments Dawlish did not think so, but he could not rid himself of suspicion. Why had Sir Jeremy come to Greyshott? If he could only prove it was really out of consideration for his nephew . . .

But then, the Croaker had possessed a similar consideration.

Dawlish said this, and more, to Rawling, Beresford, and Cutter, who were waiting at the flat. He did not tell Beresford that Joan was being watched, for he was inclined to think that the homely man's reactions would be violent. He told them the rest, particularly the affair of the shooting at the Yard, and there was the same thought in all their minds.

Morelli.

She had made an impression, and whether she was heartless or not, murderess as she was, Croaker's chief *aide* and a thousand other things, there was something about her which made it almost impossible for them really to dislike her. In fact, they wished they could see some way in which she could escape from the consequences of the Faversham murder.

But there was none, and they knew they were being fools.

Dawlish felt better as they started the dinner which Cutts and Tony had foraged, and by the end of it he felt more or less normal. He telephoned to the Yard to make sure the code had not been deciphered.

The experts, said Trivett, were still working on it.

"Experts!" scowled Dawlish. "I'd sell them. You'll ring me the moment anything turns up?"

"I've told you so a dozen times, man; be patient."

"All right."

Dawlish replaced the receiver, and at Beresford's injunction he hit the hay. Beresford, Cutter, and Rawling, all tossed for the privilege of keeping awake for the first two hours to listen for the telephone or the front door. Cutter won, and grimaced with disgust.

The others turned in, and silence fell over the flat, a silence that seemed to hum. Cutter was thinking a great deal, and wondering whether Dawlish was really worried about the possibility of Sir Jeremy being the Croaker, or at least connected with the Croaker.

Well, it would all work out. Cutter grimaced and picked up an evening paper, but as he read the sporting columns the face of a girl persisted in intruding. The face of Morelli.

It was queer that Dawlish and the others did not know her other name. Just Morelli and the Speaker, who had a loyalty that seemed absurd, but which was in reality something wonderful. Cutter scowled again, and managed to keep the vision from his mind until one o'clock. He called Beresford then, and Beresford waited by the telephone while the others slept.

No news came.

Dawn, the late-December dawn—it wanted three days to Christmas Day—was breaking through the window of the flat when Dawlish woke up, like a giant refreshed, and rang the bell for tea.

They were bathed and shaved when the telephone rang with a startling clarity. The men were reading various papers and grimacing at the sensation—for the murder of two M.P.'s, a millionaire, a pitched battle in Essex, and a killing at Scotland Yard were almost more than any respectable paper could take in one morning. They jerked their heads as though with one accord, and then Dawlish stepped to the telephone.

"Trivett!" he said, and then: "Yes?"

"We've got the code solution," said Chief-Inspector Trivett in a strained voice. "The money's at the Towers. Yes, Sir Jeremy's. And your uncle's shaken off his trailer."

27

The Towers Again

Cutter, Rawling, and Beresford stared at their friend as he took in Trivett's words, and wondered why the expression of despair crossed his face. He looked like a man who was getting the worst news he had had for a long time, and he swallowed hard once or twice. Then his voice came, very clearly:

"That's certain?"

"Yes. Are you coming?"

"I am, but don't wait."

Trivett hung up. Dawlish replaced the receiver slowly and looked at the trio. His smile came slowly.

"Uncle Jeremy after all, and he's slipped his guard. The boodle's down at the Towers."

Beresford stared.

"My dear Pat, it *can't*———"

"It can," said Rawling in that unexpectedly deep voice of his. "We've wondered, Cutts and I."

"Before last night?" asked Dawlish heavily.

"Almost from the start. Certainly since we got away from the Magpie. And remember, his voice is odd. Up and down a great deal, and when he's on the bass note he croaks. Doesn't he?"

Rawling was speaking more lengthily than usual, and Dawlish drew a deep breath. Of course this was true. And Cutter and Rawling had guessed the truth. No wonder Cutter had been disgruntled, no wonder Rawling had said very little all along. And neither of them had mentioned a word of their suspicions.

Dawlish made a queer noise in his throat.

"Well, we're going to be in at the kill."

"Why not call it off?" asked Cutter. "If the police get him there and he puts up a fight you might have to——"

"I've an idea he'd find it amusing," said Dawlish. And then he snapped: "Ted, phone for your car. The senior's spare Daimler will do. Tony, slip into my bedroom and get the guns, will you? I dropped them there last night."

He stopped speaking, and Cutts, with his hair so carefully plastered over his bare cranium, and his genial face usually serious, eyed his friend without speaking. Dawlish forced a grin.

"Not so good, Cutts. But what I can't think of, damn it, is why *Morelli* sticks by him. Jeremy's seventy. He was boasting of it only the other day. Seventy—gouty—crippled—rich. There's no sense in it."

"There's no sense in Morelli being what she is."

"But an old man and a girl like that—it's obscene."

"It might not be—what it looks to be," said Cutter soberly. "She might be a niece. Even a daughter. Illegitimate, if you like: he was a gay blade in his younger days, wasn't he?"

"No, but I've heard rumors of a *grande passion*." Dawlish spoke very seriously, and for a while he brooded. And then, for the first time that Cutter or any of the others had ever known, he helped himself to a small whisky-and-soda half an hour after breakfast. He seemed brighter after that and more boisterous, but there was no doubt what the news meant to him.

Nor was there time for thinking.

The Daimler, lent by the obliging Beresford *père,* was outside the flat fifteen minutes after Ted had telephoned, and the three of them were downstairs waiting for it. Beresford took the wheel and ignored certain regulations, but the whole of London seemed to be breathless that morning, and even a zealous traffic cop took no notice of a car going down Piccadilly at forty-five miles an hour.

Dawlish was glancing, when they had to stop, at the placards, and hearing the newsboys bawling, seeing the little groups of people gathered together and talking. The affair at Greyshott was almost a second-best to the four murders.

The incredibility of the whole thing caused the greatest effect. A useful man on the *Daily Wire* had managed to get a great deal from the Yard, and to guess more. The duel between two rival crime organizations, each headed by well-known and educated men, took hold of popular fancy and played ducks and drakes with it. But the star sensation was Morelli's.

To make it worse, a newspaper had managed to get or fake a photograph, and it was plastered on placards and in headlines—everywhere. The Faversham murder was the *pièce de résistance,* and every news editor had realized it. Morelli's name was on everyone's lips, far more than the Croaker's.

But when Sir Jeremy Pinkerton's name came out . . .

Sir Jeremy was a lover of many things, and chiefly of his own opinion. He had been featured in the papers for this opinion and that on national crises, and he had never failed to differ from the orthodox. He was not exactly a playboy, but he was looked on by the public somewhat affectionately as a diehard of the diehards. And now this. The Croaker . . .

As they neared the Towers the road grew almost congested, and the police were obviously prepared for another Greyshott massacre. If Sir Jeremy was anywhere near the Towers he would never get out.

Would he be there?

And would Naida Pelisse be with him?

Dawlish believed La Grana had found that other code, and that she was capable of trying to get after the money. He did not doubt for a moment that she had known something of her husband's activities. She might have wanted him dead simply because he was her husband, but there might have been the money angle to it as well. He wondered where she had gone after the Greet Club raid.

Beresford spoke suddenly.

"If La Grana's there with some friends as well as the Croaker, it'll be a do. All right, Pat?"

"Right as rain. First turning on the right, Ted."

Beresford took the turn to the right, through the drive gates of the Towers. Still the policemen were in evidence, and police cars littered the drive. Dawlish thought fleetingly of Morelli, and half wished she had the same chance as his uncle of making a getaway. How was she this morning?

He did not have time to inquire of Trivett, who was on the steps of the house. The Daimler had actually passed all but four cars, all containing men from the Yard, and little had been done yet. Morely was there, pale but determined.

"So the impossible has happened," Dawlish remarked.

"I'm still trying to believe it," admitted Morley. "Where's the likeliest place to find the hoard?"

"In the vault, Trivett knows that."

"A big place?"

"Pretty large."

"Any passages?"

Dawlish scowled, and scratched his blond hair.

"You mean unknown ones? Not"—he grinned—"to my knowledge. I've heard no rumors, either. There is a passage from the vault to the moat—the moat's mostly covered in now, of course—but it's been blocked ever since I can remember."

Morely looked thoughtful.

"Do you know where it should lead to?"

"Yes." Dawlish hesitated for a moment, and then looked round. "Cutts, you know the old moat entrance?"

"I do," smiled Cutter, for he had lived next door to the Towers during Dawlish's youth, and Beresford had spent a great deal of time three miles due north of the Pinkerton residence.

"Fine. Ted, you and Cutts take Trivett—unless you're going, Morely—along there. I take it you'll have a crowd, in case of accidents?"

"I'll station a dozen men and a machine gun," said Morely, and there was no possible mistaking the grimness with which this affair was to be taken by the police. "Trivett, take Munk and look after it. You'll come downstairs, Dawlish?"

"Yes. You've got the keys?"

"The butler's getting them."

"He's always slow," said Dawlish with a grin at the thought of the outraged Parsons. Parsons would never believe this of Sir Jeremy, even if Sir Jeremy admitted it. "We'll go up and help him find them. Although, of course, Jeremy might have taken the lot."

Morely nodded. Dawlish started toward the stairs, talking as he went.

"You've men stationed by the vault?"

"I'm not playing at this thing," said Morely irritably. "We're handling dynamite, Dawlish, and a man guilty of a hundred murders and God knows what else. The vault's surrounded. We're only waiting for the keys."

"I'd like to make sure," said Dawlish. "Let's hurry. Any gelignite or dynamite if the keys are missing?"

"Yes."

"All right, we'll hope for the best."

But hoping for the best wasn't good enough. Parsons, stout and dignified as ever, was standing helplessly by a small safe in his room on the top floor—where, Dawlish reminded himself grimly, he had once proposed to send Brenner and another wounded Croaker's man—and muttering to himself.

"I can't think where——"

Dawlish snapped:

"They've gone?"

"I could swear I put them in the safe before I went to bed, sir, and the safe hasn't been forced. What Sir Jeremy will say I don't know, and what he will say to it all I . . . I *beg* your pardon, sir?"

Dawlish turned with Morely from the room. They hurried down again, Morely snapping instructions for dynamite and a fuse to be used on the strong-room door.

"This'll drive anyone inside out," said Dawlish. He was trying to keep on top of himself, for he was still hating the thought that Sir Jeremy was the Croaker. "How long, Morely?"

"A three-minute fuse, I expect."

The police drew back from the door of the vault as the fuse burned, spluttering, toward the dynamite. Everything had been done in the most matter-of-fact manner possible, but there was an electric tension about the place, and Dawlish wanted to shout or sing.

He waited tense-lipped, after making sure a message was sent to Beresford and Cutts about the dynamite, and that the police watching the possible second exit were prepared.

One minute to go.

The fuse was crackling and spluttering, the little red spark gleamed brightly in the gloom.

179

Thirty seconds. Twenty. Ten.

Dawlish held his breath, and the others did the same. There was a moment of intense silence and then came the *boom!* as the thing happened. The very floor seemed to rock, there was a flash of fire that seemed to fill the cellar, a sudden rumbling of falling masonry, for the door was a foot thick and a normal charge would not have affected it. And then the light of torches began to play and Dawlish and Morely, with a dozen policemen, started to go slowly toward the gaping hole of what had once been a door.

Dawlish's lips were dry, but his fingers were very firm about the butt of his gun. He hardly knew what to expect, but he was ready to shoot on sight at anyone who loomed out of the darkness of the vault.

No one came.

The stones were tumbling, but less regularly now, and the uproar had subsided. A single electric bulb, left in its socket by accident, had remained alight. Others were fitted in quickly and the interior of the first section of the vault, where Trivett had visited when the last attack of the Croaker's on the Towers had been made, seemed empty.

Then Dawlish caught sight of the man in the second section, and he raised his gun, while Morely muttered under his breath.

"Don't kill him!"

28

Getaway?

Dawlish did not have a chance just then.

His finger was on the trigger when the man moved. Dawlish could only see his back, but the fellow half turned as he ducked behind a beer barrel or a wine cask and dropped out of sight. There came the *crack* of a shot and a bullet hummed past Dawlish's head.

The A.C. dropped behind another cask. Dawlish uttered a word of command and the police dropped down on their stomachs, guns ready.

Fierce exhilaration surged through Dawlish. The fight against the Croaker was really near its end now, but the chances were that he—and the police—would win. He ought to be dead, but he was still here, gun in hand, picturing the veined face and rheumy eyes of Sir Jeremy Pinkerton.

Sir Jeremy had not fired, but a short, stocky man, who fired again. A regular fusillade started, and the police returned the fire.

"There must be half a dozen of them," Morely muttered.

"And there'll be a way out all right," said Dawlish grimly.

"It's lucky you mentioned passages. I hope the Croaker doesn't use gas."

"*Gas!*" Morely choked.

"That's right, anticipate it." Dawlish was crawling on, with the dank smell of the vault in his nostrils. At the far end it was difficult to see, for the lights had been switched off at the first shot. But there was enough light to see the figure that suddenly darted from cover and tried to get farther down the vault. Dawlish's gun cracked and the man's cry echoed.

"One," said Dawlish. "Who's for a buggy ride?"

No one answered, but a dozen policemen crawled forward. One of them raised himself to his knees and wished he hadn't, for a bullet clipped his ear.

"They didn't expect us," Morely said oddly.

"Probably they did, but we came too soon. I wonder if La Grana is here?"

"Who?"

"Lady Pelisse. Where's your education? I wonder whether they've started to try and get out the other way yet? I wonder whether the boodle is really here, or whether they've moved it and this is just a blind?"

Dawlish's gun cracked again, and he was shooting well on the mark. The bullet hit the leg of the man who tried to cross the vault, and he pitched forward, screaming. And then another scream came, a woman's this time, and her cries seemed to raise the hair on the back of Dawlish's head.

"Stop—stop—*stop!* I can't stand it—I can't!"

La Grana!

"Hold it," snapped Dawlish. The men behind him obeyed, but no one raised his head. The footsteps came pattering through the gloom and the near silence, and suddenly Lady Pelisse came into sight. They could see the tears streaming down her face, could hear her sobbing. She was waving a handkerchief, the signal of surrender.

He raised himself cautiously, but no bullet came, and he grabbed La Grana's arm. She stumbled to her knees, still sobbing, and Dawlish's eyes were very close to hers. He was satisfied. There was no imitation hysteria here; she was beside herself.

"Steady," he said, and his voice seemed to soothe her.

He slipped a whisky flask from his pocket.

"Try a sip of this; it'll help."

"Do you know the Croaker?"

"Yes," said Dawlish ruefully. "I know, and you don't need telling I'm surprised. Where is he now?"

"Somewhere—outside," she gasped. "I saw him, with that——"

But she broke off before she had finished, for there was a sudden furious outburst of fire from the far end of the vault. Suddenly daylight streamed in, it seemed from nowhere. Three men came running back toward Dawlish and his friends, three men with guns and firing as they came. Dawlish found one and the policemen the others, and then Cutter and Beresford and half a dozen men from the Yard came up, gasping. Dawlish could see them twenty yards away, and he knew that the passage to the moat still existed.

And the Croaker was somewhere outside; La Grana had seen him.

"Where was he?" he asked, and she knew what he meant. She opened her lips, and then Dawlish saw the tall, thin, weedy man named Percy rushing toward them, merging with Cutter and Beresford's crowd. He saw the guns, the flashes of flame, and he heard La Grana gasp.

That was all.

It was so sudden that he hardly realized what had happened, but La Grana slumped forward against his chest. His arms went about her automatically, and his hands found wet blood on her back. He stood biting his lips; then swore.

"Get the tall man!"

Percy, gun in hand, made a dash for the far entrance, and

Beresford and Cutter fired at the same time. He dived forward, gracefully yet horribly, and he did not die as peacefully as La Grana.

Dawlish felt sick.

Two more were dead, two more players in this strange game. But the Croaker was still free.

The Croaker. . . .

Was it Sir Jeremy?

Reason and evidence told him that it was, but still he found himself clinging to a possibility that there had been some mistake. Why, if it was Sir Jeremy, had the weedy man shot La Grana? Supposing Lady Pelisse's lover had been the Croaker.

But there was no time for supposing.

Cutts and Beresford were with him, and Morely with Sergeant Munk and Trivett. As far as they could see there were only policemen on their feet, with Dawlish's friends. When all the lights came on a moment later they proved it.

Sir Jeremy Pinkerton certainly wasn't there, dead or alive.

There was breathing space, and all of them were grateful.

"Well, Pat? A few more," Beresford remarked.

"It's a devil. No one escaped your way?"

"They tried to and failed. I wonder where the hoard is. Or hasn't anyone thought of looking for it?"

There was a general laugh.

They needed a breathing space, and for five minutes they stood about and smoked. Morely's expression was difficult to assess, but Dawlish could guess what he was thinking.

The Croaker must not get away.

But Sir Jeremy was missing, they had no idea where he was, and they had only the dead Naida Pelisse's assurance that he was about. Trivett was glowering, but he accepted a spot of whisky from Dawlish's flask.

"Shall we clear the mess first, or start looking for the money?" Trivett asked.

Morely drew a deep breath.

"Search first; I'd like to make sure that stuff is here."

Trivett nodded, and called Munk. Dawlish watched the search, feeling too lazy to join in. When they found the jewels and the gold it would be an anticlimax. It would be a much better finish if the stuff were missing, but he seemed to expect it to be found.

Trivett located the gold, and swung on his heel with his eyes blazing. Munk yelled. Morely and Beresford with half a dozen policemen hurried to the spot, and Dawlish was on their heels.

Any lingering doubt of Sir Jeremy's guilt disappeared from his mind a few minutes later. For the bullion was stored away in a recently built chamber in the large vault. The door was unlocked, and the key was still in the hole. If the police had been half an hour later getting the message decoded the stuff would probably have been away.

Damn it, the Croaker almost deserved to win.

It seemed impossible to Pat Dawlish that he could really feel anything in common with the Croaker, but he admitted to himself in that moment that he was desperately anxious that they should never catch the old man. If he did not turn up there would always be a shred of doubt as to his guilt, and Dawlish was prepared to believe it.

Morely's voice was squeakier than usual as he talked of the gold. Trivett's beam was nearly as wide as Munk's. Never had Munk seemed so genuinely pleased with life, and prepared to admit it.

"Over a million pounds' worth," opined the sergeant, "and maybe more. All we want's the sparklers now, Trivvy."

Morely heard the "Trivvy" and ignored it. He was prepared to overlook any breach of discipline in these circumstances. Only the Croaker was missing, but a huge proportion of his loot over the past two years was here. It was the biggest recovery of stolen goods that the police had ever made or were ever likely to make, and he felt like singing. Dawlish, seeing it, knew that the man was drunk with excitement after that grim duel in the vault. When he cooled down, Morely—and for that matter all the others—would see things in a better perspective, and would realise the horror of the murders and the shooting.

Dawlish knew that his own spirits were still low because he could not rid himself of a picture of Sir Jeremy's veined face and Morelli's loveliness. Surely Morelli and his uncle could never have been associated.

Trivett's voice broke the near silence again.

"Another chamber, sir. Over here."

Morely broke off from a talk with a Yard superintendent and hurried toward Trivett. Dawlish went, more because it was all he could do. Cutter and Rawling followed him, while Beresford, for some unexplained reason, stayed near the gold. Gold, it seemed, had some fascination for the big man with the homely face.

Dawlish thought grimly that it was certainly fortunate the Croaker had not used gas. In that vault it would have been a massacre. He bent low to go into the chamber—the second new one that had been built in the vault—and as he went inside, blinking in the glare from a powerful lamp, he heard Trivett's cry, and Morely's:

"We've got him!"

And a moment later he saw Sir Jeremy Pinkerton lying on the floor of the vault, absolutely motionless, and with his face turned toward the ceiling.

So he was here.

29

Last Sortie

Dawlish stood there towering above the others as they bent down and staring at his uncle's red face. The eyes were closed and his mouth was a little agape, but he was breathing. Trivett shot out his right hand and smacked the baronet sharply on the right cheek. Pinkerton's head moved, and Trivett would have repeated the blow, but Dawlish suddenly pulled Cutter and Munk aside and knocked Trivett's hand away.

"That's enough; he's right out."

Trivett colored and would have made a comment, but he understood what was worrying Dawlish, and drew back. Morely looked uncomfortable as Dawlish turned to him.

"There's your plaything," Dawlish said oddly, and he hardly knew why he felt so bitter. Perhaps because after that fight Sir Jeremy had been caught like this, obviously the victim of one of his own men. The police usually had the luck.

"Get him upstairs," said Morely, his voice lower than usual. "I'll make sure he's looked after, Dawlish. You'll stay here and help to get this stuff out."

"This stuff" was in two opened boxes the size of small suitcases, and Dawlish saw it for the first time. He caught the glittering of the fiery facets of the diamonds, the luster of the pearls, the green glory of the emeralds, and the lambent blue of sapphires. But he glanced only once: they were an anticlimax.

"What do you mean?"

Morely looked awkward, and then Dawlish suddenly understood what the other man was afraid of. For Dawlish still had his gun in his hand, and Morely had been thinking that Dawlish might prefer to end this affair with a bullet. It would certainly be easier for Sir Jeremy.

More: Morely might still be wondering about Dawlish.

Dawlish chuckled, and slipped the gun into his pocket.

"Right! Who's in charge?"

"Superintendent Block," said Morely, obviously relieved. "Thanks. I think the jewels had better go first, Block, in a car with one in front and one behind. Take them to the Yard. We'll need vans for the bullion, but it can be taken outside. It's clear out there, isn't it?"

"It was five minutes ago," said Block, a short and chunky man.

"We'll see that it is now," said Beresford.

He had come from his gold in time to see Dawlish's expression when Sir Jeremy had been found. Cutter and Rawling went through the supposedly blocked-up passage from the vault to the side of what had once been a moat. The fresh air cheered Dawlish, and something else made him laugh.

"Your family's faithful, Cutts!"

Five or six of Cutter's friends of the gymnasium were there, and only Eric was needed to make it a perfect party.

But if Dawlish was amused the police took exception to it, and the ex-fighters were shifted quickly. Dawlish went with them and the others toward the gates of the Towers.

He had not had time yet to work the whole thing out in his mind, but knew that once his sickening sense of helplessness was gone he would feel much better. He hoped Eric would pull through. He wondered why he had not recognized Jeremy's voice through the microphone—loudspeaker, dammit—at the Magpie. It had been distorted, of course.

He recalled that the police had discovered that the man must have spoken from a room at the pub, but Sir Jeremy had managed to get away without arousing any alarm. That reminded him that he didn't understand why Morelli had been allowed to roam about Greyshott.

"There it goes," said Ted Beresford, breaking across his friend's thoughts. "A cool two million, I'd say. And Munk is making sure he goes with it."

They were at the end of the drive, and almost out of the grounds, and they could see the three cars coming along. Munk was in the first one with three policemen, the second contained Superintendent Block and three other reasonably high officials of the Yard—and the jewels. The third car was a hundred yards behind, catching up quickly.

Dawlish saw the men from the gymnasium eyeing the cars, and then saw four of them—there were eight in all—move into a touring car standing near the drive but in the road. It happened very quickly, very slickly, but he was wide awake and he snapped to Beresford:

"Jump a car, Ted. Boys, be ready for——"

What he was going to say was never heard, but Beresford just had time to reach a police car, standing idle near by, as the thing happened.

The first escort car swung through the gates, and as it came one of the ex-heavies flung a small bomb at the driver. The car didn't turn right or left but plunged into the hedge on the far side of the road. The jewel car swung right, with Munk's gun showing, but the ex-boxers showed guns too and used them. Munk went down, two others with him, and the ex-prize-fighters made for the car.

And then the next thing came with a devastating suddenness and a horrible finality—or so it seemed.

The gates and the drive just behind it seemed to lift upward. The explosion came very clearly, and the air was filled with billowing smoke and other things. The second escort car took it amidships and went sky-high, and the damage to the drive made it impossible for another car to pass.

And the raiders were on the way with the stolen jewels!

There were a dozen policemen near by, hurt or safe, but there was nothing they could do, the cars were gone. The first car with the four ex-boxers was a hundred yards from the drive gates, the jewel car was twenty yards behind it with a man at the wheel—a man who had forced open the window at the Magpie on the occasion of Dawlish's visit!

And Dawlish's borrowed car was third, with Beresford at the wheel.

Beresford lacked some things, but he could work miracles with a car and he did now. He roared onward, while Dawlish, Cutter, and Rawling waited tensely, crouching down to avoid shots that would surely come. In sixty seconds the Towers were out of sight and only the three cars mattered.

Dawlish hardly knew what he was thinking. He did not know whether these were the Croaker's men or whether it was a surprise sortie by men who liked money, but he did know it had been carefully arranged. The front of the drive had been mined . . .

What did it matter? The chase was on for two carloads of crooks and a million pounds' worth of jewels, and Dawlish behind them. The anticlimax of the whole affair and the importance of Sir Jeremy's part in it disappeared. Dawlish's eyes were gleaming and his blond hair streaming behind him as Beresford trod on the throttle and the police car showed its paces.

Eighty-five-six-seven. They were going faster every second and the two cars in front were moving as fast, along the narrow country road with the three engines roaring, and the whole countryside listening to the blare. Now to the right, now left, swinging wildly, bumping the sides, there seemed no end to the risks they had to take to keep the jewel car in sight.

The firing had not started.

Dawlish's gun was ready, Cutter's in his hand. Only Rawling had not drawn his gun, and his face was pale. But there was a glint in his eyes as they roared along, and he seemed to be smiling.

Still no firing.

And the attacking car was getting nearer. Cutter stood up slowly, steadying himself with his left hand and firing with his right. The first bullet missed: so did the second.

"Steady," urged Rawling; "it's too far off."

Dawlish agreed and Cutts held his hand, but his eyes were blazing and this time he seemed to have no presentiment. Still the cars in front went on, as though they had no idea they were being followed. Dawlish had expected a fusillade by now.

Ninety-one-two-three.

Faster, faster, the cars hardly holding the road, taking bends on two wheels and looming this side and that. Their breath seemed knocked from their bodies and how Beresford held on was a miracle, but he didn't let up for a moment. Only thirty yards behind the two cars now.

Dawlish snapped:

"Let 'em go!"

But even as he spoke he saw the other cars slowing down and caught a glimpse of the main road ahead. *And* of the bus standing at the corner of the road. The cars could not get past without crawling. Thank God for the bus!

"Hold it, boys; we'll rush them!"

As Beresford slowed down, using gears and brakes, Dawlish leapt out of the car and went rushing towards the ex-fighters. They were out too, standing by their car—*without guns in their hands.*

This was fantastic.

"Put 'em up," he said, and the four thugs from the jewel car obeyed. So did the four in the leading car. They were like candles snuffed out at will, and all their faces were bruised but blank. It was more than fantastic.

Beresford reached his friend and Rawling followed. Cutter had caught his coat in the car door but yelled to them to go on. He was grinning all over his ugly face and the wind was ruffling his sparse hair so that he proved quite bald in patches. The eight ex-toughs stood like statues, and Dawlish was wondering where the catch was. He noticed the bus was empty. Or looked empty. Was someone crouching beneath the seats?

"Watch the bus, Ted," said Dawlish, but before Beresford could go forward something made them stop, just where they were, facing the eight ex-boxers of the Aldgate Gymnasium. And a voice came from behind them, *a croaking voice!*

"Drop those guns."

It was obscene. It was impossible, for only Cutter was behind them, unless the man had spoken from behind the hedge. But there was a menace in the voice that prevented them from throwing an immediate challenge, although they all held onto their guns.

"Drop them," croaked the voice behind them, and Dawlish could stand it no longer. He swung round on his heel, and as he did so a bullet flashed from Cutter's gun and sent Dawlish's flying from his hand. *Cutter's gun!*

"Drop—them!" croaked Wishart Cutter, and the expression on his face had to be seen to be believed.

Three men like statues, with their hands by their sides but their guns on the floor, and Cutter, the little ex-lightweight, the man Dawlish would have trusted with his life, staring at them with his lips twisted and his expression grotesque. And he was talking in that incredibly obscene croaking voice.

"Clever, Pat. Ted. Tony. I will include you all. I thought you had me beaten, but luck turned. Understand?"

"Good—God!" cried Dawlish, but he didn't move.

Cutter smiled again, and it looked as though he wore a mask. "Yes, I'm the Croaker. I tried to fix it on Sir Jeremy, but it didn't come off. You came after my men. Know why they didn't shoot now?"

Dawlish muttered:

"You—swine!"

"I shouldn't say that," said Cutter, croaking unbelievably. "I did all I could to save you. If you hadn't kept up with the hare so well you'd have been all right. And so would I. I will be still, Pat. Because I've got to shoot you this time. And leave you here. My chaps will go off in the bus, and the jewels. I'll be here, looking a mess. The only one of us left alive after another battle. I've been working this for a long time, Pat. The Magpie was my idea. The gymnasium my official headquarters. Most of the men my men. Understand?"

"I'm beginning to," Dawlish muttered.

"You may as well, but we mustn't be long. I used the Croaker's men to help you against the Croaker. Twisted humor, my dear Pat. And you understand now why so many men got in and out of the Magpie without 'seeing' anything. You can understand why none of us suffered at the Magpie. You can understand why I was 'shot' on the drive last night at Greyshott. I didn't want to be in the house. If you hadn't got Morelli—and I'll never forgive you for that, the place would have been blown sky-high. But I wanted to save her. Anything else?"

"You——," swore Patrick Dawlish, and he leapt forward: and as he went guns leapt like magic into the hands of the thugs behind him.

193

30

Windup

Dawlish thought of nothing but the things he had heard and the incredible presence of the Croaker in front of him—or, rather, of Wishart Cutter. He could believe more readily that Jeremy Pinkerton was the Croaker. Disgust and contempt for Cutter outweighed the discovery that the man was the Croaker, that a friend of his could be.

Cutter pressed the trigger of his gun, and Beresford gasped. But there was an empty click, and Dawlish in a wonderful moment realized that Cutter had emptied his gun in mock firing at his own men. As the thought came Dawlish was on top of his man.

Cutter hurled the empty gun, but it flew past Dawlish's head, and they crashed down. There were a dozen shots, but the thugs stopped shooting, for Dawlish and Cutter were rolling over on the ground and a bullet might hit either of them. But when Beresford moved, his face working, a bullet took him in the leg and he went sprawling. Tony Rawling just stood and stared, knowing there was nothing he could do and praying for just one thing.

That Dawlish would finish the Croaker.

Nothing else mattered, for there seemed no chance of living now, the odds were helpless. If the Croaker were killed, the ex-fighters would shift for themselves, and they would not leave anyone alive to tell the tale.

Three men went forward, hulking, brutish specimens, toward the fighting, kicking men on the ground. Dawlish was on top most of the time, but the Croaker had great strength for a little man. Now three guns were raised, waiting for an opportunity of shooting Dawlish. And Tony Rawling had to stand, with five guns pointing toward him, watching. His lips were working, he wanted to close his eyes, he . . .

"Gentlemen!" said the voice from behind him.

It came from behind the thugs too—a light, feminine voice —and Rawling thought he was imagining things. But as he swung round he caught a glimpse of the girl, standing very slim and straight and with the automatic in her hand.

Nor were the men behind her the Croaker's men. They were mostly in uniform and looking very capable, while those who did not have automatics held rifles. And they moved forward, with the ex-boxers backing away with eyes wide, and the two men struggling on the ground as though they were fighting for life and death.

Until the Croaker took a punch from Dawlish beneath the chin and jerked back, dead out. Dawlish stood up slowly, painfully, prepared for a bullet. Instead he saw the men in blue, and what struck him as most incongruous—the weirdest thing he had seen for many a day—Ted Beresford with his arms round Joan Fayre and laughing as though he would cry.

Joan Fayre was talking quickly. She was excited, and small wonder; but Dawlish, Beresford, and Tony Rawling could have listened to her forever.

"It was that big man who was shot yesterday—Eric," she said. "He telephoned me, but how he knew where I was I don't know. He told me that the bus would be here, that I must tell the police I knew they wouldn't believe him, so I told them, and——"

"Here we are," said Dawlish, pushing his hair out of his

eyes. He looked a mess—a very red mess; but he felt on top of the world. "Joan, you're the loveliest creature I've ever set eyes on. Did Eric say how he knew?"

"No, he just told me exactly where the bus was to be."

Dawlish was on top of the world as they reached the Towers in the cars which had run that chase through the narrow country lanes. In the leading car were two policemen, Ted Beresford, and Joan Fayre. With Dawlish was another policeman, Tony Rawling, and the Croaker—still unconscious, but bound hand and foot. No one proposed to take chances.

The Croaker was alive, and somehow Dawlish expected that he would tell the truth before he went for the long drop; there were several things Dawlish wanted to know. Before he learned them, however, he enjoyed the sight of Trivett's face, and Sir Archibald Morley's, when they arrived with their prisoners; for the bus was following the cars with eight handcuffed men inside.

"How's Jeremy?"

"In his bedroom, conscious and swearing he knows nothing about it," said Morely. "He's been so convincing that I half believed him, and yet it didn't seem possible."

"Cutter told me he'd planted it on Jeremy," Dawlish said, "and we'll soon find out how. I'll go up."

Dawlish, feeling absurdly light-hearted, hurried up the stairs. He found Sir Jeremy Pinkerton with three police sergeants in the room, and he heard him swearing. As Dawlish entered the baronet jerked up on his pillows.

"Come in here, you young fool, and start talking. Who says I'm the Croaker? You, I'll wring your neck! Tell that stuffed nincompoop downstairs I'll have him drummed out of the Force, I'll have his hide! I'll ruin him! Me—the—Croaker!"

The three sergeants eyed each other, for Sir Jeremy was certainly croaking. But Dawlish was beaming, and he grabbed Sir Jeremy's right hand.

"It looked bad for you," he said; "but it's all right, we've got him."

"What's that?"

"We've got the Croaker. My friend Cutter."

"*Cutter!*" Sir Jeremy looked dazed for a moment, and then his veins swelled out and he spluttered viciously. "The—little —swine! He asked me to let him work on some experiments in the vault. And some scientist friends of his. I'm not using the big vault, only for a cellar, and—and I let him! I let him!"

"And you explain a lot," said Pat Dawlish gently. "Now take it easy, Pinky, and lie down."

Dawlish was right when he said that the baronet had explained a great deal, and later the Croaker confirmed it. The Croaker talked like a man who was half-crazed. But he talked, and that was the main thing.

He had obtained Sir Jeremy's permission to use the vault, and he had built extra chambers inside for storing heavy valuables. It had been a fairly easy task, for most of the servants were in his pay, and the bricks had been brought through the moat passage entrance. Then had come the Croaker's biggest double cross. He had persuaded Pelisse to store the Greet syndicate's boodle at the Towers.

For Pelisse had believed Cutter to be working for him!

That was true, and Morelli afterward confirmed it. The Croaker had inveigled himself into Pelisse's confidence, and he had seen nothing to stop him from getting away with the syndicate's cash. He had killed Pelisse as soon as the job was done —after Pelisse had heard rumors of a raid on the Greet Club —and he had used La Grana and her Percy as a false lead for the police. He had twisted and turned to keep suspicion from himself; and until he had gone to the Towers on the final day no one had known him to be the Croaker except Morelli. But he had disclosed his identity to the ex-boxers he had massed there, and explained the trick to come, if possible, with the jewel car.

La Grana, Lady Pelisse, had overheard him, and would have told Dawlish. But the Croaker had shot her, while the others had believed it to be the weedy Percy, and the Croaker had silenced Percy while making it look as though he was working so hard for the police party.

His reward to Sir Jeremy had been a blow over the head because the baronet had gone—by chance—to the vault, and Sir Jeremy was lucky it had not been a bullet.

All these things had been necessary because the Croaker had made one big mistake. He had gambled with his money on the Stock Exchange and lost heavily, and only the syndicate's cash could make him financially sound. So that he could work without being forced to cover his movements in England, he had officially gone to America. But actually he had been in the East End, perfecting his organization, getting into Pelisse's confidence, doing a hundred things.

And but for an accident no one could have avoided he would have succeeded. A prop in the old passage of the vault had given way, and it had taken the Croaker's men—servants of Sir Jeremy's but in the Croaker's pay—two days to put the trouble right. But for that there would have been no need even for the Greyshott affair; but delay had been dangerous, and the police as well as Dawlish had been threatening.

"Why didn't you put a bullet through our heads?" Dawlish asked; and the Croaker, still in that dazed fashion, stared at him.

"Well—we were friends. I didn't want to kill you. I got worked up after I heard where Morelli was. And I would gladly have murdered you at the coach. But apart from that I would have rather you lived."

Wishart Cutter drew in a choking breath, and then turned

his head, dropping forward in an attitude of utter dejection. That was the last Dawlish saw of him, for two days afterward, in the same cell at Brixton, the Croaker was found hanging, with torn pieces of a sheet making a noose.

Sir Archibald Morely looked steadily at Dawlish, and then pressed a bell on his desk.

"I want you to meet Superintendent Larsen of the Manchester division," he said, and Dawlish knew the other thing was now in the limbo of forgotten things. "Specially drafted from Manchester to work on the Croaker case. No one at the Yard knew it but myself, which explains why he used Miss Fayre to send a message. Ah, come in, Larsen!"

And *Eric*—spruce, smiling, and very self-possessed—entered the room and shook Dawlish's hand, and apologized for his grip. The wound in his shoulder, he said, still hurt, but the wound in his forehead was mostly imaginary.

They went out together half an hour afterward. Eric's quiet soothing voice, Eric's rich laugh, Eric's warm friendliness—Dawlish was intrigued and said so. Eric was an ex-heavyweight who knew how to use his fists and had scented the lead at the gymnasium. He had managed to get out of hospital on the morning of the Towers' affair and get to the Croaker's headquarters. A sergeant, equally unknown to the Croaker, gave him news of the bus assignation, and Eric had telephoned Joan Fayre.

"She'll want to meet you," Dawlish said. "She's due at my flat any time, with Ted and Tony. Care for a bite with us?"

"Try and keep me away," said Eric Larsen.

As they went toward Clarge Street they talked of the many queer things in the Croaker case. Of the Pelisse domestic tangle which had given many false scents and which the Croaker had used—although Percy was not in either organization, and had gone to the Towers at La Grana's exhortation, because La Grana thought she could get some of her husband's hush-money. Of the dozen scents that had tailed off to nothing, of the many men and women who had belonged to one organization or the other, and who were now free—but probably innocuous—and most of all of Morelli.

But at the flat, an hour later, Joan Fayre was the toast of the evening, while outside the newsboys were screeching of the second prison suicide that week, and at the Home Office some august gentlemen were saying it was perhaps as well.

Thereafter the party grew gayer. Beresford was limping from his wounded leg, it was true, and Dawlish had three punctures, but none of them severe, with a nose more battered than usual. But they had escaped more lightly than the police, and had learned with delight that Sergeant Munk was not too badly hurt.

"Of it all," Dawlish said, more lightly than he really felt, "the affair at the Magpie worried me most. It was uncanny. But Cutter *was* uncanny. He had an opportunity for talking through some blasted microphone—that right, Tony?"

Rawling, the mechanic of the party, agreed.

"I thought it was," said Dawlish genially. "While you—and I—were looking for him. Well, it's over and done with and I wouldn't like to repeat it. But I wonder," added Patrick Dawlish, "whether they'd like me for a policeman?"